HIS QUEEN OF CLUBS

RENEE ROSE

BURNING DESIRES

Copyright © June 2019 His Queen of Clubs by Renee Rose

Published in the United States of America

Renee Rose Romance

Editor: Maggie Ryan

This book is a work of fiction. While reference might be made to actual historical events or existing locations, the names, characters, places and incidents are either the product of the author's imaginations or are used fictitiously, and any resemblance to actual persons, living or dead, business establishments, events, or locales is entirely coincidental.

This book contains descriptions of many BDSM and sexual practices, but this is a work of fiction and, as such, should not be used in any way as a guide. The author and publisher will not be responsible for any loss, harm, injury, or death resulting from use of the information contained within. In other words, don't try this at home, folks!

ACKNOWLEDGMENTS

My enormous gratitude to Aubrey Cara for her beta read and for Maggie Ryan's editing. You are the best!

Thanks also to the amazing members of my kinkster Facebook group, Renee's Romper Room.

If you haven't joined yet, **what are you waiting for? Email me** with your the email address you use to log into Facebook and I'll invite you to the secret group.

CHAPTER 1

 *lad*

NO FUCKING WAY. Just when I thought I was the least lucky bastard on this continent, I catch a break.

I've been staking out the Bellissimo and Nico Tacone for two months now.

The Tacones took down my entire cell. Junior Tacone and his brothers destroyed the Chicago operation while I was back in Moscow dealing with my mother's affairs. Granted, Ivan, my idiot second, planned to take them all out and forever end their reign of influence in the Windy City. But he failed. And six of my men were found dead in an Italian cafe.

Victor put Ivan in charge of setting up the street business, but he was too small-minded and power-hungry to make it into much. And when I was sent to join the cell, he saw me as a threat to his autonomy. I had set up a meet with Junior to get the Tacone family involved in my laundering scheme—to diversify interests—but Ivan fucked everything up. When my mother died and I had to fly home to Moscow, he used my absence to try to eliminate the Italians and take the Chicago underworld for himself.

He underestimated Junior Tacone. Six of our guys ready and waiting with guns, and Junior single-handedly shot them all dead.

I'm not heartbroken over the loss of the Chicago business. I'm more concerned with the big money operations of the *bratva*. I'm the guy who manages our laundering accounts. But killing all the men in my cell? Unacceptable. And Victor, our *pakhan,* ordered me to exact revenge, so I'm here to do exactly that.

The Tacones may have done the brotherhood a favor by taking Ivan out, but they still owe me.

Victor would go for blood. Kill everyone Junior Tacone loves. That's the way he operates. But I'm not that guy. Yes, I was raised in the violence and death of the organization, but I'm the money man.

And the Tacones have money. Plenty of it.

But it's not coming from their Chicago operation. As far as I can tell, they'd begun shutting down most of their loan sharking on the streets in the past few years, and completely closed shop since I've been back.

So I came to Vegas. Where they own one of the most lucrative casinos in the country. And I've been watching the two Tacones who run it, trying to figure out what my play will be. I was thinking about taking one of their women. Simple ransom. Both men are clearly devoted to their wives—girlfriends—whatever.

And things just got much easier for me. Two limos rolled up this afternoon carrying the entire Tacone family—the three brothers from Chicago, a girlfriend, a mother, and a beautiful young sister in her early twenties.

I got a gossipy cocktail waitress to tell me everything she knows. I found out they're here for Junior Tacone's wedding—a spur of the moment kind of thing. The entire top floors of the casino have been closed off for the celebration. Rumor has it Stefano, the youngest brother, might marry his fiancée at the same time.

But I don't give a shit about their marital status.

All I care about is one Tacone.

The lovely Alessia—baby sister to all five multimillionaire brothers. I'd been trying to figure out which female to take—which brother would be most willing to pay for his woman. Now it's easy. Grab the one they all care about.

And I don't mean the mother.

Of course my decision to take Alessia over the old lady has everything to do with her model-perfect body, mile-long legs, and fucking gorgeous face. If I'm going to hole up with a Tacone female, it might as well be one who's worth looking at.

All I have to do is knock out one of the waiters before he brings the food up to the wedding celebration and take his uniform and his place.

~

Alessia

. . .

MY BROTHER JUNIOR is the biggest *stronzo*.

Actually, all five of my brothers are assholes, but Junior's the worst. He informed us this morning that he and his pregnant girlfriend were going to elope in Vegas.

Tonight.

Which meant we all had to fly to Vegas to see it.

Although, honestly, I wouldn't have missed this moment for the world. Even if traveling means a lot of work keeping my mother happy and my blood sugar under control. And it makes it harder to hide the fatigue caused by my kidney condition from my ever-watchful family. They don't know about it and that's how I'm going to keep it for as long as possible.

We're up in one of the Bellissimo's top floors, in a reception area with wall-to-wall windows overlooking Vegas. There's a Catholic priest here to marry them. And the event turned into a surprise double wedding.

Stefano, my only easy-going brother—which doesn't mean he isn't just as lethal as the rest of them—popped the question to his girlfriend Corey this morning and they decided to make it a two-fer.

"Mary, Queen of Peace, pray for us," I murmur and cross myself in unison with the rest of the attendees and the priest.

I can't believe Junior's remarrying. Well, it's not the remarrying part that shocks me. It's the happiness that radiates from him now as he stands facing Desiree, his tough-as-nails bride. He holds both her hands in his, gazing at her like she's his whole world. Beside him stands her young son. Watching Junior's quiet bond with him brings me to tears. Junior lost his preschool daughter in a tragic accident years back and shut down completely. I never thought he'd open his heart to love again. Now he's not only got a baby on the way, but he's doing the stepdad thing.

"Isn't it beautiful?" my mom whispers tearily, squeezing my hand.

"Absolutely perfect," I agree, crying right along with my mother.

Nico's pregnant wife Sondra went all out on the decor. The hall must have ten thousand dollars worth of flowers. The pillars and real grape vines draping over the trellises make it feel like we're back in the old country.

Tasteful and extravagant, yet also low-key, the ceremony fits both couples. Only forty or so family members fill the place. It's made all the sweeter by the two pregnant bellies—Sondra and Desiree are both expecting.

I'm so thrilled to be an aunt. Children are my passion —I got my degree in early childhood education, even though I'll probably never be allowed to work. Not by my family. Not by whatever husband my family chooses for me.

It stings knowing I'll never have any of this—the love, the impromptu elopement, a family.

The expectation was always for me, as the Family princess, to endure a huge virginal church wedding to some Made man of my father or brothers' choosing. No staring into the eyes of a man who loves me. It would be an arranged marriage all the way.

I used to fervently wish for a love match. Back when I thought I'd actually marry and have children of my own. I was overjoyed when Nico got away with marrying a woman of his own choosing instead of the bride he had been promised to from the time he was ten.

I've been allowed some freedoms I never thought I'd get.

They let me go to college. I had to campaign for years just to get Junior to consider it, but in the end, he relented. The diabetes almost kept them from letting me go, though. They see me as fragile. Mamma didn't want me out of her sight. My brothers didn't think I could handle myself.

They wanted me to stay where they could protect me—in either Chicago or Las Vegas.

But in the end we all compromised. They sent me to university in the Old Country where I could be watched over by *La Famiglia*. The Sicilians. And my brother Stefano was there part of the time, too, to keep a very close eye on me.

I'm always guarded like a princess in a convent. Which doesn't mean I didn't sneak in a few experiences. I stole kisses with a nice Italian boy who took my V-card in the most respectful way possible. But when he found out I was part of the Family, he couldn't run fast enough. Which was just as well, because I wouldn't want him to be hurt.

I was just looking to live a little before it's too late.

Because what my family doesn't know is that I'm in stage three kidney failure as a result of the diabetes. I've been told having children would kill me.

So the love match and babies of my own isn't ever going to happen.

In fact, if I don't take care of myself, I may not live to see twenty-five.

Vlad

I RETURN to the Bellissimo with a plan and everything I need to execute it: A syringe filled with tranquilizer. Rope to tie her wrists and ankles. Tape for her mouth. Mikhael—Mika, as we call him—my twelve-year-old accomplice and the only living member of the Chicago *bratva,* to drive the getaway car.

I get off the elevator wearing the crisp Bellissimo waiter's uniform, pushing the cart I plan to carry the girl out in.

I leave the cart just outside the door and stand in the doorway, scanning the room. I keep my head down and my tattooed fingers clasped behind my back. If the Chicago-based Tacone brothers recognize me, I'll be a dead man before I can take a breath. Not that I care. If I were overly-worried about living long, I wouldn't be here. Ironically, it's my carelessness with life that always makes me come out on top.

I take risks. I'm never ruled by fear. I saw the way the *bratva* worked early on and figured out how to come out on top. I made myself indispensable. Not through violence, although I've had my fair share, but through knowledge.

I learned how to hack. How to launder. I learned to speak English, German and French. That's how I won control of all of the *bratva's* money. How I amassed a fortune. How I survived countless attacks against me. If the shit with the treacherous Sabina hadn't gone down, I'd still be on top there instead of lying low in America.

7

I make a mental note of every weapon-bulge in the room—at least twenty-four. Every man there is carrying a piece—even the grooms. Instead of fear, the familiar buzz of adrenaline sets my skin tingling.

A surreptitious scan of the room and I find the mafia princess. The one I will use to bring every Tacone to his knees.

The one who will learn a little humility at my hands.

I should hate my enemy's sister—should consider her an enemy too, but it's hard to hate any creature so beautiful. And it's not her fault she was born into a ruthless family.

The Italians keep their females pure. The women never participate in business. Never see blood or death.

Hell, the girl may even still be a virgin. *Blyat*, now my dick's hard. Now is not the time to get a stiffie over the woman I plan to drug and tie up. Except I'm a sick motherfucker, because that thought only gets me harder.

She's wearing a hot pink halter dress that frames and presents her youthful breasts in the most mouthwatering way. The matching pink shoes and purse probably cost a grand alone.

Fortune's smiling on me, because Alessia breaks from the group and heads for the door, like she's going to the restroom.

I move swiftly, pushing my cart into the hallway behind her, palming the syringe. I remove the false top of the cart, revealing the empty bottom, which is actually one of the Bellissimo's rolling laundry carts.

I wait until she emerges from the restroom—alone, thank fuck—and jump her from behind. If she were a man,

I would just knock her out with my fist, like I did the waiter downstairs. But I can't bring myself to hit a woman, no matter how easy and effective that might be.

I catch her vanilla and roses scent as I cover her mouth and jab the hypodermic needle into her neck. She struggles against me as the drug moves through her veins. It will take at least a minute to take effect.

"Shh, *printsessa*," I murmur in her ear, keeping my grip across her arms and over her mouth, iron-tight. "Relax and you won't get hurt." My accent sounds thicker than usual. Probably because my cock just got thicker at the feel of her soft ass wriggling against it. "Easy, *zaika*. Go to sleep."

Her intoxicating floral aroma fills my nostrils as I breathe into her neck, waiting. Finally, she goes limp, her supple body sagging in my arms.

I swoop an arm under her knees and drop her into the cart, then put the top back on, arranging the tablecloth over everything. Twenty-nine seconds later I'm in the elevator. One of the Tacones' men gets on with me. I keep my face blank, but formal.

The guy doesn't look at me. I palm the knife in my pocket, ready to use it if I have to.

Finally, the guy gets off on a lower floor and a few other people get on—tourists. Nobodies. I hit the door close button and continue downstairs to the lower level.

I text Mika, *On my way*. I try to use English with him, so he'll learn to read and write it.

In position, he texts back in Russian. I shouldn't involve the kid in this shit. Hell, I shouldn't have even brought him here from Chicago. But what else was I do with him? I came back from my mother's funeral in Moscow to find six of the brotherhood dead and everyone else gone. Everyone except Mika.

He'd been living alone in the apartment building we occupied, somehow surviving. Probably a greater kindness would've been to give him to the American social care system. But I couldn't do it. He may be an annoyance, but he's one of ours, and we take care of our own. And he's working hard to prove himself useful.

In the lower level corridor, I strip off the waiter suit and put on a maintenance staff button down shirt, pull the catering top off the cart and roll it out, like I'm taking out dirty laundry. I wipe my prints from her purse and toss it in the trash.

Mika pulls around to the door and stops with a jerk. Yes, I let a twelve-year-old drive my car. I didn't even have to teach him—he already knew how. And he's damn good at it.

"Open the trunk," I mutter to him in Russian and he complies as I push the cart right up to the back of my black Jetta. I pick up the drugged Tacone princess and drop her into the trunk, then slam it shut.

Twenty-three seconds and we're out of there.

Mission accomplished. I now have all the leverage I will need against the Tacone pricks.

CHAPTER 2

 *lessia*

I FEEL LIKE HEAVING. As light filters under my lids, I remember being captured. The sharp jab of a needle. The thick, strong arms banded around me. Tattooed knuckles pressing over my mouth. The heavy Russian accent. Hot breath at my ear—not unpleasing, even though it terrified me.

I'm so fucked.

I try to blink my eyes open, but they won't obey. I'm shaky and black swims over my vision. My heart's racing but I can't wake up. Cold sweat makes my dress cling to me. I don't know if it's whatever he injected me with dragging at me, or if I'm heading toward a diabetic coma. Either way, I'm screwed.

I force my mouth to move, to ask for help.

If I can't wake up now, I may never wake up again.

∽

Vlad

THE GIRL SHOULD BE awake by now. I'm not on expert on narcotics, but I've seen this concoction used before. I researched how much to give her, and I doubt I guessed far off on her weight.

I have her bound on the bed in the upstairs loft of my rented townhouse. Mika stands in the doorway, kicking a hacky sack back and forth while I check Alessia's pulse. It feels weak and erratic. I grip her face and turn it from side to side, trying to make sure she's not faking it. The way her head lolls tells me she's not. Her lids flutter open, but all I see are the whites of her eyes, like they're rolled back in her head.

A shot of pure alarm makes my heart pound.

"Alessia. Wake up, *printsessa*." I lightly tap her face. "Wake up."

Her lips move but I can't hear what she's saying.

"What's that?"

She mumbles something flops her hand at me and that's when I see the medical bracelet. It's rose gold and expensive-looking so I didn't notice the symbol at first.

Fuck.

I flip it over to read what it says.

Diabetic.

Double fuck.

With my phone, I Google what to do in the case of an emergency with a diabetic.

Fuck. According to the screen, she needs emergency medical care, and I'm not about to surrender her to the local hospital. If the girl dies, she's absolutely no use to me. And I don't want her death on my conscience. I already have far too many.

I disposed of her purse in case they could track her by her phone, but now I'm kicking myself. I shout to Mika to bring me a can of Coke from the kitchen.

When he brings it, I tell him in terse Russian, "I need you to drive back to the casino and get her purse. I threw it in the trash can outside the elevators and in front of the door where you picked me up. It's very important—could mean her life. But don't get caught. Understand?"

He's frightened by my tone, but he nods quickly.

"You can do this, Mika. Call me if you can't find it."

"I'll find it," he says, throwing a frightened glance at the girl tied up on the bed.

"And don't bring her phone with you! Leave it in the trash. Just the purse and the rest of the contents, okay? Go quickly, now."

Mika agrees and dashes off.

I crack the can and scoop under the girl's shoulders to prop her against my body. "Drink, *zaika*." I attempt to dribble Coke from a can into the mafia princess's mouth.

Diabetic.

I never saw that one coming.

The Tacones are so perfect, so wealthy. The girl is so beautiful; it's like I didn't think something like illness or ill-fate would touch them.

But of course, sickness is immune to wealth or power or even beauty.

Fuck. For some reason, her handicap makes it much harder for me to hate her. And I was struggling as it was. It's hard to hate the beautiful. It's like someone not liking a puppy or kitten.

It's almost hard to believe how perfect her face is. Full, bow-shaped lips, thick, slightly-arched brows, long lashes. Her olive skin is flawless and smooth.

Alessia's lids flutter and her lips move against the can. She swallows. "Yes," she murmurs, acknowledging what I'm trying to do.

"Good girl."

I keep at it for an agonizingly long time. Waking her from her faint, trying to get the sugary substance down her throat to bring her blood sugar levels back up.

"Mika's picking up your insulin, *printsessa*," I murmur as I dribble more Coke down her throat. "You're not dying today."

She makes a sound as she swallows. She understands me. Knows what's going on here. Her attempts to open her lids are getting more successful. Her eyes track my face, brows dip.

"Why?" she rasps.

"Why kidnap you?" I don't know why I'm inclined to make conversation with her. She doesn't deserve any politeness or special handling from me. But it's like it's impossible not to answer. "Your brother killed my cell."

Her eyes drift closed again.

I put the can to her lips again. "Drink. You're no use to me dead."

She mumbles something, her full lips wet with the amber liquid. I want to lick the sweetness from them. Bite those lips. Punish her for being a Tacone. For being so beautiful. "What's that?"

"Fuck you."

I chuckle. "You still have a little fight in you, hmm? Good. I liked wrestling with you back at the casino. Made my dick hard."

Her eyes fly back open, pupils narrowing in fear as soon as they land on my face.

I give her a wicked smile.

She blinks several times, but it seems to take too much effort to keep her eyes open, because they roll back and she slides back into a faint.

Oops.

The adrenaline spike she got from my taunt probably wiped her out.

I'm a sicker fuck than I thought because even with her passed out I want to fuck her.

Hard.

Rough.

I want to ride the mafia princess until she screams and begs me to let her come.

It seems to take forever, but finally I hear Mika's footsteps racing up the stairs.

"I got it," he says in Russian, holding the pink purse. "No one saw me."

"Good job."

I dump the contents on the bed. Lipstick, wallet. A syringe and bottle of insulin falls out, along with a test kit and a piece of paper with hand-written instructions taped to it. *If unconscious, administer glucagon.* The glucagon is in a red kit labeled with the same black Sharpie. Instructions inside have me mix the powder with saline in the syringe. As I work, I bark orders at Mika. "Check the bag for an electronic trace. It could be something small and thin, like a watch battery."

I follow the instructions and pinch the skin of her belly, jabbing into the fat layer and slowly pushing down the plunger on the syringe glucagon.

I check my watch. How long will it take? How long does she have before her body shuts down completely? I don't know enough about diabetes to know what I'm dealing with here.

"Nothing," Mika reports.

I search through everything on the bed. The contents appear to be innocuous.

"Give it to me." I hold my hand out for the purse. Nothing changes in the boy's face—the kid is always stoic as fuck, but somehow I know I've offended him. "I trust you, Mika, I just want to double-check." I point to the stuff on the bed. "You double-check my work here."

The boy nods and moves to the bed, picking up and looking over everything the way I had.

He's not a good kid. I'm not sure he even has a moral compass. I've seen him beat boys twice his size on the street for no reason at all. He's dangerous as hell.

But like a feral dog who finds someone to feed him, he's bonded to me. He'll do whatever the fuck I say without question. Kidnap a woman and tie her up on a bed? No problem.

Drive a car to the enemy's lair? Whatever you say, boss.

And as much as I know I'm doing him a disservice, I don't trust him with anyone else. I know he's broken. His bitch of a mother made sure of that… Junior Tacone completed it when he orphaned the kid from his *bratva*. I have little to offer, but at least I will give him his dignity and the skills to survive.

Alessia stirs. Her eyes open.

Thank fuck.

She groans and rolls to her side. "I'm going to puke."

It takes me a moment to translate the word puke, but the look on her face helps. "Mika, hand me the trash can," I order in Russian.

Mika moves quickly, his intelligence and reflexes perfectly honed for emergencies. The kid has probably been through too many to count. A girl puking is nothing compared to what he's seen.

I get there just in time for her to lose her lunch in the wastebasket.

Mika makes a sound of disgust.

"You can go," I dismiss him.

It's not because I want to be alone with the girl.

Yeah, right.

I want to strip the girl bare and tie her up to this bed. Taunt her with my cock and record her pleading.

Instead I get a wet washcloth and bring it to her. And because her hands are tied, I wipe her mouth with it.

She glares at me. We're close. I loom over her, checking to see if there's anywhere else to clean. Her focus

17

falls to my tattooed knuckles, follows the ink on my forearms, stops at the bulge of my biceps.

She swallows.

I sprout a chub. Does she find my strength attractive? The way her pupils dilate makes me think she does. But then, who knows if she's ever been close to a man who wasn't her brother before.

"You could've killed me," she accuses.

I allow one corner of my lips to lift in a humorless grin. "I still can, *printsessa*."

I watch a ripple of fear run through her and she attempts to scoot up to sitting without the use of her hands. I let her struggle, enjoying the way her fuchsia dress rides up her ripe thighs. Her legs are long, lean and strong, her calves shapely. Somehow the heels are still on.

She licks her lips and my boner grows. "I need to check my blood sugar."

Alessia

"THIS?" The Russian picks up the tester kit. I blink, getting a better look at him now that I can focus. He has sandy blond hair, piercing blue eyes and multiple scars on his stubbled jaw. He's wearing a plain white t-shirt that stretches over his bulging muscles and his arms and fingers are covered in tattoos.

Unfortunately, I find his look sexy. He's the modern

James Dean bad boy. Or the street version of actor Jeremy Renner.

I'm both terrified and turned on by him at the same time. Maybe it was just feeling all that raw masculine strength when he grabbed me. Maybe my hormones are on full blast after watching two of my siblings tie the knot.

My captor cocks his head and raises a stern brow.

"Yes, that. Untie me."

"Oh, *zaika*. Let's get one thing straight right now. You're not giving the orders here."

I shouldn't find his thick accent sexy, either, but I do.

I give it right back to him, arching my own brow. "You need me alive. That means keeping my blood sugar stable. So untie my hands and let me test my glucose."

"Nyet."

Such a final-sounding word, the Russian *no*.

He examines the glucose meter, figuring out how it works while I watch without offering any help. He's not a dumb man, though. He picks up the lancet. "From your finger, I presume?"

I don't answer.

He grips my bound wrists and tugs one of the fingers away from the rest. His touch isn't cruel, but I choose this moment to make my dissatisfaction known, and I use both hands to punch him in the nose.

Well, punch is a loose description. I can't really punch with my wrists bound, nor can I wind up to make it effective. I sort of knew that before I tried, but figured it was still worth it as an act of defiance.

A signal of war.

I don't break his nose. I don't even make it bleed.

Cristo, I'm not even sure I hurt him, but he reacts quickly, swiping my hands down and pinning them to the mattress, effectively dropping me to my side. He looms over me, eyes glittering.

Oh fuck.

Is he excited?

Too late, I remember his warning that he was turned on by wrestling me.

And my foolish body reacts, heat pooling between my legs as if this is some kind of mating ritual, and not a brutal kidnapping.

All right, maybe not that brutal.

"Don't hit, *zaika*. You won't like the punishment."

Why does the word *punishment* get my feminine parts tingly?

I lick my lips. "What is it?" I shouldn't give him the satisfaction of asking, but I do.

His smile is wicked. He removes one of my pink pumps and tosses it to the floor. "Strike me again, and you lose your clothing privileges. The dress comes off, *printsessa.*" He removes the other shoe. I become distinctly aware of my damp panties and the fact that there's only a thin piece of fabric between my pussy and those rough hands.

A slow throb starts between my legs, my nipples tighten. Fearing a hard blush come on, I speak quickly to distract myself and him. "What is *zaika*?"

His feral smile returns. "Bunny. Now give me your finger like a good girl."

I lift my middle finger.

His eyes glitter, like he loves my challenge. A ripple of

sexual tension hits me full blast when he holds it and jabs the tip with the lancet, then squeezes a drop of blood onto the test strip. He inserts it into the meter and turns the screen to show me the readout.

"Still too low," I tell him. "I don't need insulin."

He examines a hypodermic needle and a bottle of insulin. "When you do need it, where do you take the shot?"

This time I definitely flush. "You can give it in my arm."

His eyes narrow as he recognizes my discomfort. "Where do you usually take it?"

I lift my chin. "None of your business."

One corner of his mouth lifts. "Your ass?" he guesses.

"My belly!" I snap.

His eyes gleam and he reaches for the hem of my dress. "What, *zaika*? You're afraid I'll see your pink panties?"

Heat flushes up my neck to my ears as he slowly drags the hem up, exposing my thighs, then my panties, to my belly button.

He runs the back of one knuckle across the front of my panties, sending tremors down my inner thighs. "You think I didn't already see these pretty things when you were in my trunk? Or tied up on my bed?"

My stomach flips. Oh *Santa Maria*. This is his bed? I am so screwed.

Maybe the full reality of my situation finally hits me. Maybe good sense returns and fear sets in, but for whatever reason, my eyes suddenly fill with tears. I lock away, blinking. Pissed that he saw he got to me.

He cups my jaw. "Don't cry. It you behave, you won't get hurt. It's your brothers I want to punish, not you."

I meet his eyes, surprised at the sudden change in his demeanor.

He drops my chin and walks away, giving me his back.

I close my eyes, blocking out the sight of him. Of this room.

Of my new prison.

 *lad*

"WAIT."

Shit. I need to get away from this woman. She's too much of a temptation. I could look at her face all day and never grow tired of it. She's that beautiful. And her beauty does stupid things to me. Like make me want to be nice.

And there's no fucking place for nice here.

Worse, I don't just want to look at her face. I want to bite those lips, fuck that mouth, watch her eyes roll back in her head when I pound her hard.

And I'm not going to do any of those things.

I don't rape women.

I may not trust women. I may think they are manipulative liars who want to lure you into their lair and eat your heart out. But I still wouldn't take what wasn't offered.

I may make the little mafia princess *think* I'm going to, but I wouldn't do it.

"What?" I don't bother turning around.

"I have to pee. And I'm hungry."

Fuck. I rotate and pin her with a hard stare.

A blush creeps up her neck. She may pretend to be tough—and I love it when she does—but I know the truth. She's afraid of me.

And a little turned on.

"Okay, *printsessa*. Get up."

She raises her brows and attempts to shimmy toward the end of the bed.

I watch for a moment, because it's so fucking hot the way her dress rides up and I sure as hell want to see those pink panties again.

When she finally makes it to the edge of the bed, I walk over and untie her ankles.

"Go." I lift her to her feet and slap her ass, hard enough to be a warning.

She squeaks and scuttles forward, then turns and holds out her bound wrists to me. "What about these?"

I shake my head. "Make do. Bathroom is there. Leave door open." Her nearness thickens my accent, makes me drop the article before *door.*

"Fuck you," she mutters as she moves away.

I smack her ass again.

Damn if she doesn't toss her long thick hair and swish her hips as she crosses the room to the bathroom.

Adorable.

The girl is seriously something.

Definitely my lucky day. The Tacones couldn't have given me a better gift than their beautiful, fresh-faced sister.

I go still, a prickle racing across my skin as a thought occurs to me.

No.

It's a terrible idea.

I lift my eyes to Alessia, who compromised, leaving the door open six inches. Good. She knows I'll carry out my threatened punishment.

I return to my terrible idea. Could I?

Probably not.

Should I?

Definitely not.

My burner phone buzzes. It's Victor, my *pakhan.* The papa, or big boss of our *bratva.* The one who sent me away after Sabina pulled her tricks. He's the only one who has this number, seeing as how it's a new phone.

"*Da, Pakhan.*"

"Come back. Zima's dead," he says in Russian.

Zima's the reason Victor ordered me to leave. Zima wanted me dead. Victor wouldn't allow it. As the *derzhatel obschaka*—the bookkeeper of the organization—I'm too valuable to him. Or maybe it was out of respect for my mother, his long-time mistress. Either way, I was banished. Sent with the brigadier Ivan to set up a cell in Chicago. A shit job, and one I'm totally over-qualified for. So I let Ivan have his fun and kept working on my laundering schemes.

The toilet flushes from the bathroom.

My heart pounds with the audacity of my idea.

"*Da*. I'll come right away. As soon as I get the paperwork in order to bring my new bride. I'm taking the Tacone girl as my own. They'll pay me to keep her alive and well. It's the very best revenge."

Victor doesn't speak for a moment. Marriage is forbidden as part of the thieves' Code of Conduct, but one that involves revenge on an enemy is a different situation.

"Good. I want you here by Sunday. Business has become sloppy without you."

"I'll see you Sunday, Papa."

He ends the call without a goodbye as I continue to stare at the bathroom door. When Alessia emerges with another haughty toss of her hair, my dick lengthens down my pant leg.

Yes.

No better way to fuck the Tacones up the ass than to marry into their family. Claim their baby sister as my bride and demand payment in the form of a dowry.

To keep her in the style she's accustomed to, of course.

Not that I don't have plenty of money already.

No, this is business. I'm marking my territory in the cruelest way possible. Making that link I was trying to forge before—between American mafia and Russian.

And claiming the most spectacular trophy possible in the process.

Alessia Tacone, my bride.

"Come."

Alessia

THE RUSSIAN BECKONS ME OVER.

I want to refuse, but I'm afraid of what will happen. The guy seems sane enough, but that doesn't mean he's not dangerous. Especially if he has a beef with my family. I don't doubt what he told me.

That my brother—I don't even know which one, but it doesn't matter—it could've been any of them—killed everyone in his cell.

That's not something I would ever want to know my brothers did, but the truth is, I know we're mafia. I know violence happens. Probably way more than I want to think.

So I'd probably be wise to cooperate a little with this guy until my brothers get me out of here.

I walk to him, not missing the way his gaze skims over my body. I'm in a dress that clings to my curves in a color that lights up my face. Taking advantage of his veiled appreciation, I thrust out my bound hands. "Alessia Tacone. And you are?"

"Vlad," he says easily.

The fact that he's unafraid to share it with me sends warning tingles up my spine. Either I'm not getting out of this alive, or he has no idea that Sicilians don't rest until they've taken vengeance.

Of course, I'm his vengeance on them.

He wraps his tattooed fingers around my upper arm and leads me to the door. "Move, *zaika*."

"Where are we going?"

"To the kitchen. For food."

27

I walk down the stairs of what is actually a beautiful townhouse. Light-filled and airy, the living room has a lofted ceiling and a state-of-the-art television on the wall.

I'm surprised to see a boy in desperate need of a haircut perched on the back of the expensive leather couch with his feet on the cushions watching Disney Channel with his head cocked to the side. He turns to look at me, his expression guarded.

The teacher in me is horrified to find a child in this situation. He's witnessing a felony kidnapping, becoming acclimated to violence and crime. The worst part of it is that he doesn't even seem frightened or disturbed by it.

"Why do I get the feeling this isn't his first rodeo?" I mutter, more to myself than to Vlad.

"It's not."

Vlad leads me through the living area to a small but finely appointed kitchen, where he pushes me into a chair at the table and ties my ankles to it.

"Is he your son?"

Okay, now that I've seen the boy, I'm less certain of Vlad's sanity. Who, in their right mind, involves a kid in an abduction? Why isn't the boy in school? What in the hell is going on? My passion for children surges, and the need to interfere rises to the surface.

"No."

The boy looks over, like he's listening, and he and Vlad meet eyes briefly, before the boy drops his.

"Mika is an orphan, thanks to your brother."

I draw in a sharp breath, my ribs constricting painfully. I know I hid my head in the sand all along about family business—that was what was expected of me. But this is definitely not something I wanted to hear. Ever.

I blink back hot tears.

Vlad stares at me, the intensity of his gaze searing through me.

"I'm sorry." I meet his eyes evenly to show him I mean it. The tears brim but don't fall.

A muscle tics in his tight jaw. "I believe you." His voice is gruff. He turns on the oven and pulls a frozen pizza out of the freezer.

I know I'm a prisoner here, but he wants me alive, so I speak up. "Vlad, I can't eat that."

He looks at the pizza, then back at me. "Why not? The diabetes?"

I nod, not wanting to mention the kidney stuff. I try not to think about it. "I love pizza and pasta and bread, but I have to stick to low carb foods like meat and vegetables."

He tosses the pizza onto the counter and opens a cabinet. He pulls out a can of sardines. "Low carbs. Okay." He cracks open the can and gets a fork.

"What do you know about your brothers' business?" He unwraps the pizza and puts it in the oven without waiting for it to pre-heat.

"Nothing."

"Nothing," he repeats back in his thick accent. It sounds more like *nothingk*. "The Sicilians keep their women out of the business, no?"

"Yes," I admit softly.

He opens the refrigerator and produces a bag of baby carrots. Like a lion approaching trapped prey, he saunters over to me and holds a carrot to my lips.

I meet his ice blue gaze, surprised.

He shrugs. "I'm not untying you. If you want to eat, it will be by my hand, so you'd better learn to be sweet."

My core clenches. That shouldn't be exciting, but my body didn't get the memo. Apparently being hand-fed by a Russian mobster is a turn-on. Or maybe it was knowing I'm at his mercy. The order to be sweet.

Either way, a prickle of awareness runs over my skin, tightening my nipples as I take a bite of the proffered vegetable. The Russian stands over me, watching. I swear his gaze is hungry.

The carrot is delicious, or maybe I'm just starving. I swallow the bite and lift my lips for more.

The hardened lines of his face soften as he feeds me the other half of the carrot, then pulls out another. "You know nothingk, so I will tell you. Junior shot and killed six of my men in a restaurant called Caffe Milano in February."

I stop eating, my appetite suddenly gone.

"You know it?" he asks in a fake conversational tone.

"And who shot my brother?" I demand. February was when Gio got shot. When Junior refused to take him to a hospital and instead brought in a nurse to care for him at home.

The nurse he just married today.

Fresh tears sting my eyes thinking of how their wedding must've been ruined by my kidnapping. How worried they all must be over me.

"If you think my brothers won't kill you for this, you're mad."

He shrugs. "Oh I'm sure they'll want me dead. But they won't do it."

I dread the answer to my next question. "Why not?"

The feral smile plays over his lips. He feeds me another carrot. "Because, *zaika*. I'm not giving you back. And they won't want you harmed, see? Plus, it will be very hard to find us in Russia."

Russia.

Not giving me back.

Full-on panic blooms in my belly, floods my body with adrenaline. I attempt to surge up from my chair, which only succeeds in rocking it forward and throwing my chest into the table.

Apparently unimpressed, he tips me back with a nudge to my shoulder.

"I'm not going to Russia with you," I tell him. Like saying it firmly enough will make it so.

"You are. You will be my bride, *zaika*. And you will learn to obey your husband. Be a good girl, and you may eventually earn your freedom."

My heart thunders in my chest. *"No."*

"Izvinyayus."

"What's that mean?"

"It means *sorry*. Your fate has been sealed, *printsessa*. You're mine. Your brothers will pay me to keep you."

My stomach twists in a tight knot.

"Don't worry, I will keep you well." He holds out another carrot, but I turn my head sharply away.

He catches my chin and turns my face up to his. The touch is gentle but his eyes blaze with potent command. "You *will* eat. Do not test me."

31

I glare at him, but to my horror, his handsome, cruel face goes blurry when my eyes swim with tears.

He strokes my cheek with his thumb, nothing changing in his expression.

Once more, I feel that squeeze in my core. Like my body loves the idea of being this man's prisoner, even as my mind rebels.

A tear escapes my right eye and falls onto his fingers.

He holds my gaze as he lifts his knuckles to his mouth and sucks it off. He cocks his head to the side. "Maybe I'll let you go," he says, like he's discussing where he wants to eat, not my entire future. "After a year or two. We'll see."

"Vlad, you can't…"

"Ah, but I can, *zaika*." He taps the table where the bag of carrots sits. "Enough arguing. Show me you'll be a good girl and eat." He holds another up to my lips.

I shake my head, planning to refuse. We lock gazes, his blue eyes boring into mine, and I open my mouth and eat, just like he commanded.

Damn him.

In silence, we maintain our staring contest—Vlad towering over me, hand feeding me the carrots, then the sardines. Me, accepting every bite, glaring up at him with all the defiance I dare give. All the while, my traitorous body responds to his nearness. His stark masculinity—the power behind the bulging muscles, the force of his presence.

"Good girl," he says when I finish. The oven timer goes off. He pulls out the pizza and tosses it on the cardboard box it came in. "Mika. Come."

The boy swings his legs around on the back of the

couch and jumps down. He might be younger than I initially thought.

When he comes into the kitchen, I ask him. "Mika, how old are you?"

The boy shoots a look at Vlad, who shrugs. "You can answer."

"Twelve," he mutters. He wears an angry glare, but it's not directed at me, it's toward the table.

Vlad hands him a slice of pizza on a plate and places an orange beside it. "Here you go. Get a glass of milk to go with it."

The boy obeys and I'm slightly reassured. Vlad is at least taking care of his basic food needs. But still, this boy should be in school.

"What grade are you in?"

"None," the boy replies defensively. Like he's daring me to try to make him go to school.

"You want to go back to Russia, Mika?" Vlad asks.

Fear ripples over Mika's expression and my heart squeezes. "*Nyet,*" he says quickly.

Vlad seems to understand the boy's apprehension. "With me," he clarifies. "I'm taking the girl to Volgograd."

Mika still appears wary.

"You'll stay with me, unless you'd rather I deliver you to someone else's care."

I sense reluctance in Vlad's offer, like he hasn't bought into the idea of taking care of this boy forever, but the relief on Mika's face makes me want to throw my arms around Vlad and kiss him.

Poor Mika. Newly orphaned, he's probably terrified of

being abandoned or pawned off with someone else. He just wants to bond to someone to get his needs met.

I'm suddenly not as upset about Vlad taking me to Russia. Someone needs to look after this boy, to give him an education and make sure he's cared for. If I'm along, I can make sure of his well-being. I owe it to him, considering it was Junior who left him orphaned.

CHAPTER 4

 *lad*

IN THE BEDROOM, I untie Alessia's wrists to check on the skin beneath. It's chafed and raw, so I wind a scrap of one of my t-shirts around the area before retying her.

She's quiet through it all. Withdrawn.

I pick up the glucometer to check her blood sugar before bed.

"You don't need to check again. I should be stable now," she mutters.

I ignore her and take the drop of blood anyway. She doesn't strike me as the suicide type, but I'd rather not rely on her for all my information. She's right, though, her numbers are in range, according to the range she gave me.

I make a mental note to research the hell out of her illness, so I can properly care for her.

Already a fierce protectiveness for her consumes me,

which is unusual for me. I don't trust women. In my experience, they are the most conniving, deceitful creatures under the sun. But this one happens to be completely at my mercy, which changes the dynamic significantly.

She's also beautiful.

That shouldn't matter. It shouldn't make a difference, but it does.

Of course, Sabina was beautiful, and look what she did. Nearly got me killed. I still don't know what her game was—why she'd want to set me up.

I remove Alessia's ankle ropes and escort her to the bathroom. Find an unopened toothbrush in the drawer. "You can use this." I drop it on the counter.

"How do you expect me to brush with my wrists tied?"

I shrug. "Your choice. Figure it out or don't. And leave the door open." I step out to the bedroom to give her a modicum of privacy.

She emerges a few minutes later and I tie her to the bed and turn off the light.

Then I don't know what the fuck to do with myself. Lying next to her will make my dick so hard it will break off. But I'm not about to leave her to her own devices, either.

I do a quick check on Mika, not that the kid ever needs anything. He's curled up on the sofa where he's been sleeping and watching television. I don't tell him it's lights out time. He's too self-sufficient to need that kind of shit. I just walk around and turn out lights like I do every night, leaving one on low in the kitchen in case he gets up.

"*Dobri nochi,* Mika." I reach over the back of the sofa and squeeze his arm.

"*Dobri nochi*," he mumbles sleepily and hits the off button on the remote control.

Upstairs I brush my teeth and kick off my shoes. I decide sleeping fully clothed on top of the covers is the best option. If I rub up against that soft, youthful skin of hers during the night, there's no telling what I'll do.

"What happened to Mika's parents?" Alessia croaks in the darkness.

Christ. Was that why she was so quiet? She's been thinking about Mika this whole time? A tight band squeezes my chest.

Fuck. I don't want to find this woman so damn sympathetic.

"I already told you," I snap, even though she doesn't deserve it. Even though what I told her isn't altogether true.

"Junior killed them?" Her tremulous tone forces the truth from me.

"*Nyet*. No. Boy had no father, as far as I know," I admit. "His mother was a whore for the *bratva*. She and Mika came over here with Aleksi, one of the men in my cell. Then she ran away and left Mika with our cell. Aleksi looked after him. Your brother killed Aleksi."

"His mother...left him with the Russian *mafiya*?"

"*Da*. Bitch ran off. Left her son as soon as they got to America. I guess she saw the trip as her ticket to freedom. She told Mika to be loyal to us so we'd take care of him."

The kid *is* loyal as hell. But I sure as hell didn't want responsibility for him.

"And you did?" Alarm rings in her voice.

"*Da*." It is more or less true. Training brats off the

street has long been a part of Russian *mafiya*. "I was gone when your brother killed everyone. When I came back, I found the boy surviving on his own. He'd eaten all the food in the house and was stealing from stores in the neighborhood to survive. He hid from the police when they came to search the place."

"Oh God. The poor kid." She's silent a moment. "Has he been to school?"

"No." Integrating the kid into American society was not part of my plan. He is no worse off than he would have been in Russia with his prostitute mother. His chances for survival—and even a decent living situation—went way up when he became my responsibility. I know, because he sticks to me like glue. He's grateful as hell and does everything I say without question.

"He's still learning English. And I chose to keep him with me, keep him close. It's a short-term situation."

"What's the long-term one?"

Return him to lower ranks of the *bratva*. "Haven't figured that out yet."

"You're blackmailing my family, right? Demanding money for me?"

"Yes."

"Some of that money should go to the boy." She says it fiercely, like she's prepared to fight me on this. I'd like to say I'm unmoved by her compassion for the boy, but a twisting, guilty sort of feeling moves in my center.

This woman may not be the selfish, spoiled princess I imagined her to be. She is coddled, naive and soft, though, as a sheltered daughter would be. But I appreciate her passion for the kid.

"*Da.* Okay. I will set up an account for him. Off-shore, tax-free, of course."

She rolls over in the dark, and looks up at me. I have to fight the urge to touch her. To brush that chestnut hair back from her lovely face. To run my thumb over those pouty lips. Shove it in her mouth and make her suck.

"Promise?"

"My word."

She lays her head back down and sighs.

I can't resist. I burrow my fingers into her hair and gently massage her scalp.

She makes a soft surrendering sound. I keep at it until she falls asleep.

Then I force myself to move away from her, to the far side of the bed, facing away.

CHAPTER 5

 *lessia*

"Take these off me," I moan when I wake up, my arms aching from being held in the same position too long. I hold my wrists out to Vlad, without much hope of his compliance. I am his prisoner, after all.

But he's also not a tyrant. I can see that already. He rewrapped my wrists last night when he saw the rope was biting into my skin. And he massaged my head until I fell asleep last night. I'm not sure I've ever felt anything so wonderful in my life.

I'm not sure he ever slept.

He's sitting up in bed, his clothes still on, fingers flying over the keyboard of his laptop. Funny, I would've pegged him for the hunt and peck kind of typist. I guess I misjudged.

Without a word, he reaches over and unties me, just

like that. I groan and shake my arms out, rubbing away the pins and needles before I lean over and untie my ankles.

"I want to go home."

I know I sound like a baby. And I know he's not going to say, "Okay" and send me home. But he ought to hear my complaints.

"Izvinyayus."

Sorry. I guess I'm learning Russian. I remember that one from yesterday.

He hands me a plate with a blueberry muffin and checks my blood sugar like he's an old pro. Clearly he's done some research since yesterday. The fact that he knew to have food ready for me as soon as I got up is impressive. Even more impressive is how he administers the correct dose of insulin without me telling him. Like yesterday, when he bares my belly, I flush at having my panties revealed. At his touch on my skin. The way my body reacts to his closeness.

I finish the muffin, trying to pretend I'm unaffected. When I set down the plate, he gestures toward the bathroom. "Go. Shower. Brush teeth."

I get halfway to the bathroom before I stop and turn. "Vlad."

"*Da*?"

"Are you really taking me to Russia?"

I swear I see a flicker of regret on his face before it hardens into something resolute. "*Da*. You are coming. You belong to me now."

Something flip flops in my belly. It's not just fear. It's something base and animalistic. It's awareness of Vlad's raw masculinity. His belief he owns me. Despite my anger and my refusal to submit, my panties are damp at the idea.

And that just pisses me off.

"It will be your funeral, my friend." I have zero doubt that my brothers will kill him when they find me.

And why does that make my gut tighten?

Because I'm way too compassionate. Too attachable, if that's a word. I already feel the need to shelter and care for young Mika. And my feelings for Vlad...aren't completely sour.

But that doesn't mean I'm going to let him take me to Russia.

I need to find a way to get the hell out of here. And I'm going to start by searching the bathroom for some kind of weapon.

I close the door and lock it.

Less than thirty seconds later Vlad throws the door open, filling the space with his barrel chest and forbidding visage.

A shiver runs down my spine right before he reaches for me and yanks my dress off over my head. The shock of his punishment ripples through me. I stand in my panties fighting the tremble that starts in my inner thighs.

The backs of my knees.

Up my neck.

"What did I tell you would happen if you defy me?" His accent is thicker than usual, blue glare cold.

I'll be damned if I cower for him though. I force myself not to move and lift my chin.

He grips my elbow and spins me around to face the

mirror, then puts a hand between my shoulder blades and forces my chest down to the counter.

My breasts spread and flatten on the cool marble.

"Bad bunny." He slaps my ass three times, hard. All in the same place.

Oh my God, he called me *bunny*. In English.

My stupid body thinks it's foreplay, because I totally soak my panties. I dare a glance in the mirror and tangle in his gaze. His light blue eyes appear darker. Stormy. He holds my eyes as he spanks me again.

My pussy clenches.

Cristo, this should not be such a turn on. My ass tingles and twitches where he slapped it. The other cheek wants the same treatment. Some dark fantasy of being manhandled, of being taken roughly, perhaps even forced lurks in the edges of my sexual consciousness. A desire I've never acknowledged.

A seriously twisted kink.

Vlad still hasn't released me from his gaze. He smacks the other cheek—*thank God!*—and his hand stays there, squeezing roughly. With his other hand, he cups my throat, lifts my torso until it hits his chest. He's stepped right behind me, the hard bulge of his cock pressing against my panty-clad ass.

Oh Jesus, the flutters in my belly are unreal. My breath is short and trembly. His is hot, right at my ear.

"You're down to panties, *zaika.* What happens if you disobey me again?"

Pussy clenches.

I don't answer, because it seemed a rhetorical question,

but he bites the place where neck meets shoulder. Hard enough to leave a mark.

I gasp.

"Answer me, *printsessa*."

Flutters. More flutters. Flutters all over. Everywhere.

"I-I lose my panties?"

Oh my God, I sound like the idiot heroine of a goofy porn video.

Vlad chuckles darkly. "That's right, *printsessa*. "You'll be naked for me." He eases his hips back and thrusts, shoving my pelvis up against the counter and his hardness between the cradle of my legs. "And if this is my reaction to your panties, what do you think I'll do when you're naked?"

Full-body shiver.

He shifts his hips to the side and smacks my ass again, right where I want it.

A moan falls from my lips before I can call it back. Vlad thrusts hard between my legs, his hand tightening on my neck. I whimper.

"*Blyat*," Vlad mutters. "You keep making those noises, you're going to get yourself fucked right now, *printsessa*. I'm trying to hold back, but you make it hard."

Oh, *Santa Maria*. My eyes roll back in my head. I'm so turned on, I'm drunk with lust.

His thumb traces along the line of my jaw, fingers still wrapped around my neck. "I like the way you tremble, Alessia."

I tremble harder. The flat plane of my belly shudders with each ragged breath. "Vlad," I whisper.

He thrusts against me again. "Say it again."

45

"Vlad." I'm shivering. My skin hot and tingly, pussy molten.

Vlad slides the hand at my throat down and roughly squeezes my breast.

This time I let the moan out without trying to stop myself.

"You *need* a good fucking." There's wonder in his voice.

I try to swallow, but can't. My lips open. His thumb slides in.

I bite down, hard.

He yanks it out at the same time he thrusts against my entrance again. The gusset of my panties is so soaked, I fear he can feel it through his jeans.

He pushes my torso back down and starts spanking my ass in hard slaps that rain down on one side then the other.

I moan wantonly. The pain comes as a relief. Exactly what I need to take the edge off the sexual tension threatening to shatter me from the inside out.

He doesn't hold back, either. Each swat stings and smarts and leaves me panting and oh-so-wet. When he angles his hand to swat between my legs, a mini orgasm rips through me.

∼

Vlad

THE GIRL JUST ORGASMED.

I admit I picked Alessia as my hostage because she's

easy on the eyes, but I never in a million years thought I'd see anything this hot. If I sold tickets to this show, I'd make a half million in a day. Not that I would ever, in any lifetime, allow another man to see what I'm seeing. No, I already feel fiercely possessive of her.

Alessia Tacone is the stuff fantasies are made of. She's got the face to launch a thousand ships. The body to bring a million men to their knees. And this display of wanton sexuality just forever ruined me for any other woman.

Good thing I'm keeping her.

"*Blyat*," I rasp in her ear. "You're making my balls ache so bad, they'll fall off."

Her sweet, soft body continues to tremble against mine. I want to reach between her legs and bring her to orgasm again. I know it wouldn't take much, she's still on the edge, ripe and ready for it.

But if I do that, I will end up ripping down her panties and pounding into her until we both raise the roof, and I can't do that.

Not while she's still my prisoner.

Not until she's my wife. Safe and sound at my estate outside Volgograd.

Not unless I'm sure she wants it.

I don't rape women.

So I force myself away from her and slap that delicious ass again. "Get in shower." My accent is so thick, it's a wonder she can understand me. "Leave door open or suffer the consequences."

She stumbles toward the shower and doesn't look back, stepping behind the curtain without turning on the water or taking off her underclothes.

She's so fucking compelling. It's not just the beauty, it's the mixture of ripe innocence and sass. The courage and pride, despite her circumstances. The compassion she showed Mika.

I want to possess her in every way. Spank her, dominate her, spoil her. I want her on her knees, looking up at me with those big, Sicilian eyes, eager to please.

And I'm now compelled to earn the trust that scene would require. To teach her to obey and honor me and reward her for her efforts.

Lavishly.

With orgasms, riches, attention. Praise. More orgasms.

Can I make her like Russia?

To want to stay?

Because if I don't, I already know I'd be incapable of keeping her against her will long-term.

I'll take her brother's money and set her free, eventually, if she won't stay.

But what if she stayed?

She drops her panties outside the shower curtain and I hear the water start up.

Out. Get the fuck out.

I force myself to back out of the bathroom, squeezing my throbbing dick through my jeans. I'll have to jack off before the day is through or I'll definitely be rolling her to her stomach and fucking her from behind in the middle of the night.

But right now, I have business to take care of.

Passports to make, documents to forge. Private flights to book.

I take her dress and lock it in the false bottom of my

suitcase with my other valuables, then return to my laptop. I'm almost finished altering the electronic trace for Anya Popov, Mika's mother. I've changed her age to twenty-eight and swapped her photo to one of Alessia that I pulled from her Instagram account. Girl should be more careful about her privacy settings, not that I couldn't hack them. Now it appears the bitch who came over and abandoned her son is returning to Russia, taking her son and their suddenly no-longer expired visas with her.

Hacking was a skill taught to me at a young age by Igor Ivanovich, head of the cell I was placed with when my mother became Victor's mistress. It's a skill I might consider teaching Mika. It would keep him off the street, give him a trade he can use to forge his way in the *bratva*. To make himself too useful to ever kill. And rich, too, if he's smart about it.

I have money squirrelled away in accounts all over the world, under too many names to list. I've set up elaborate money laundering schemes for the top dogs in the *bratva*, for the crooked politicians, not only of Russia, but of the Ukraine, Slovenia, and South America.

Getting money out of the Tacones isn't a necessity. It's just my preferred revenge.

Money's always been a game to me. Numbers on my screen, in my accounts. Transfers and dividends and passive income not only kept me alive this long, but made me incredibly wealthy. A wealth I mostly keep hidden from those around me, even the *bratva*. Only Victor knows how much I really have. I was transparent with him because if he found out otherwise, he would assume I'd stolen it from him.

Despite my grudges, the twelve-year-old boy in me still needs his approval. He's still the papa of the organization and of my life.

Even with my mother now dead.

The water shuts off in the bathroom. I don't let myself look through the open door, because seeing Alessia wet and naked will drive me fucking insane. Even so, my cock swells against my zipper, forcing me to shift my position on the bed.

I call a pilot I know in Ireland and make arrangements for him to be here with a private jet ready to fly out by midnight at the latest. No way in hell I'm trusting any pilot in the U.S. because the Tacones could have spies anywhere.

Alessia comes out with her wet hair falling over her shoulders and a towel wrapped around her.

I shake my head and she stops.

"Drop the towel," I growl. "You lost your clothing privileges."

Her nostrils flare. She's over being turned on and now she's pissed. "*Figlio di puttana!*"

I don't speak Italian, but I get the gist. "Watch it, *printsessa,* or I'll smack that ass red again."

Color tinges her cheeks.

My dick turns marble hard.

Damn, how I want to pound between those legs until she screams.

I clear my throat. "The towel."

She tosses her hair, sending splatters of water around the room. With one flick of her wrist, she removes the towel and throws it in my face. Lucky for both of us, she's wearing panties beneath it.

That doesn't stop my cock from throbbing.

"Over here." I sound far more gruff than I mean to. That's what blue balls do to me. I force myself to take a breath before I get near her, before I bind her wrists and tie her to the bed.

She smells like apples and honey. Is that what my shampoo smells like? It can't. I've never smelled anything so erotically alluring before in my life.

I wrap the swath of fabric around her wrists first to keep the rope from biting, then bind her hands together. I attach them to the headboard for good measure, but I leave her ankles free. It has nothing to do with me wanting to watch those long legs thrash around on the bed when she tries to move.

Nothing at all.

Fuck.

I'm not going to get anything done if I stay in this room with her. At least not anything that's not porno-graphic.

When I'm sure she's secured tightly, I get up and leave. I need to get Alessia more than just a muffin to eat.

Need to make sure Mika's had breakfast.

Mostly, I just need to get away from the temptress tied to my bed.

 *lessia*

"OATMEAL?" I ask when Vlad returns carrying a bowl.

He looks into the bowl. "Yeah? I guess." He shrugs. "Mika likes it."

That shouldn't warm my heart. Neither should the fact that he's sliced banana into the bowl and brought up a cup of steaming coffee. He looks street rough and bad boy to the core, but Vlad isn't any rougher than one of my brothers at heart.

He releases the rope connecting my wrists to the headboard and helps me sit up, propped in the middle of the bed with a pillow behind my back. He sits beside me and holds the spoon out.

"Really? You're going to hand feed me again? Don't you have something better to do with your time?"

He pauses with the spoon halfway to my mouth, like

he's really considering the question. He gives the shrug again. "Yes and no."

"Explain." I swallow a spoonful of oatmeal which actually totally hits the spot.

"Yes, I have work to do. But I can't have my prisoner slipping into a diabetic coma on me again."

"You already gave me insulin."

"I like you at my mercy."

There it is. The crux of our relationship, and I fear the source of our mutual attraction. It's sick and wrong on every level. And why I need to escape from this man's clutches immediately. Before he gets me to Russia. Before he grows on me any more.

He lifts the rim of the coffee cup to my lips and I sip it gingerly.

And nearly spit it out. "Oh my God! Is that *instant* coffee?"

Vlad shrugs. "So?"

I make a face. "Disgusting."

He lifts the cup to his mouth and drains the whole thing in one go, then wipes his mouth with the back of his hand. "No espresso today, *printsessa*."

I stare at the empty cup, my disappointment real. Yeah, I have way bigger problems to worry about—like being almost naked and tied to a man's bed. Needing to escape before he brings me halfway across the world. But that coffee had smelled good.

And I really like my coffee in the morning, dammit.

"Is that how Russians make coffee?" If he's going to call me princess, I might as well act like one.

He shoves another spoonful of oatmeal in my mouth.

"Russians drink tea. Those who drink coffee, drink instant. In general."

I realize it behooves me to keep him in conversation. The more I learn about him, the better. Also, the sooner I can get him to trust me, the quicker I will find a way to escape. No more shutting the door when he tells me not to. I need to act like the obedient little prisoner and lull him into complacency.

Contemplating obedience makes me shift my ass on the bed. The sting of the spanking has already worn off. If that's Vlad's version of punishment, I'm not in much danger of even breaking a nail. It appears he's more into humiliation than invoking real pain or fear.

Which is good, because I'm not into real pain or fear, either.

And the humiliation...was pretty hot.

"And you?"

Surprise flits over his face, like no one's ever asked him what he drinks. When he tosses a shrug, I realize it's characteristic. "I like both."

"But not espresso?" I let a teasing smile play at my lips.

I'm rewarded with an answering one that takes my breath away. He studies me for a moment, like I'm the most fascinating creature who ever walked the Earth, then feeds me another spoonful. "I never developed a taste for it. How do you like yours?"

I finish chewing and swallow. "Decaf cappuccino."

"*Decaf?*" He sneers. "What's the point?"

"The caffeine affects blood sugar more." And my

blood pressure, which isn't good for the kidney problem, but I don't like to think about that.

His face softens into sympathy. "Ah." He thumbs a drop of milk away from my lower lip. "Such a perfect package, it's hard to believe the goods inside are damaged." I flinch and he shakes his head. "I didn't mean it that way. I only lament my misconception. The mafia princess doesn't live the charmed life I imagined, that's all."

For some reason, that makes my eyes sting. Maybe because I didn't expect so much compassion from my kidnapper.

Of course, he sees it. His brows dip and he slides his thumb over my cheek. "Shhh. I'll take care of you, Alessia. I made a mistake drugging you yesterday, because I didn't know. Won't happen again. Your body requires vigilance. Maintaining a delicate balance. I will manage the diabetes. You don't need to worry anymore."

Something vibrates behind my sternum. A trembling I can't identify. My eyes grow wet, although I cannot fathom why. I've always hated my family assuming I'm weak and fragile, fussing over me, yet the idea of him taking over feels like a relief.

This man *needs* to keep me alive. He's using me for ransom money. He's not a life partner pledging to take away the burden of diabetes. Or if that is what he's doing, he's insane. He won't keep me as his captive bride. I'm not sticking around for that.

I turn my head away, refusing any more food. My stomach's too knotted to eat more, anyway.

Vlad mutters something in Russian and unceremoniously pulls me flat on my back with his tattooed fingers around my thigh. My panties ride up my ass and I wriggle, trying to get them back down.

"*Blyat*." He shakes his head and grips my wrists to refasten them to the headboard.

It's obviously some kind of curse word. I would ask for the translation, but I'm feeling too sullen.

When Vlad leaves the room, I let myself indulge in a few tears.

Vlad

I KEEP AWAY from the loft bedroom for most of the morning. The girl is far too much of a temptation to me, especially with her dress off.

Her punishment has become mine, too.

All morning long, though, her voice plays and replays in my ear. Her scent tickles my nose. I think of the feel of her silky hair through my fingers, or her pretty princess ass under my hand.

She's so enticing. So far from the spoiled brat I imagined her to be.

But that doesn't mean I can untie her. Or trust her. Or let her go.

Her brothers still owe me restitution.

Even so, when I send Mika out to pick us up burgers from In-N-Out, I have him swing through the Starbucks drive-thru for a large decaf cappuccino.

What can I say?

The girl's already under my skin.

For a *bratva* member so high in the organization, I am too much of a sucker. That's probably why Victor kept me behind the scenes. That, and as a favor to my mother. To keep me safe. Not that I didn't have my fair share of violence.

When Mika returns, I bring the food upstairs.

Alessia lifts her head up and glares daggers at me, but her beautiful dusky pink nipples are hard.

Christ, is she turned on? From being tied up naked?

I sure as hell am. My cock lunges acrobatically at my zipper.

Fuck. This isn't going to work. There's no way I will manage to feed her without first holding her down and sucking each of those taut nipples until she's moaning and wet.

I drop the food on the dresser and grab one of my t-shirts from the drawer. "I will permit you a brief outing," I say, like I'm taking her to the zoo or something.

She narrows her eyes. "Outing where?"

"To kitchen."

She snorts.

I untie her hands and inspect her wrists. I don't like there are marks, despite the padding. I rub them out to restore circulation. Then, as the tic in my cheek becomes stronger and stronger due to the proximity of her fucking gorgeous breasts, I yank the t-shirt over her head.

After I let her use the bathroom, I say, "Let's go *printsessa,*" and throw her over my shoulder. Having her walk would probably be a better choice. She could use the movement, I'm sure. But I like taking charge of her body. Showing her she belongs to me.

Fuck that, I just like touching her. Having her flesh against mine, especially in an undignified but hot position.

I carry her down the stairs and deposit her on the kitchen chair where I had her last time. I tie her to the chair with her arms free, but the rope knotted in back so she can't go anywhere and point a stern finger at her. "Don't move."

She scowls at me, pushing those pouty lips out in a way that makes my dick harder than stone. I want to push it between those full lips and gag her with my thickness.

"Mika." I call to the boy. "Watch her while I get the food." I would send the boy for the food I left upstairs but I know Alessia likes the boy.

I know. I'm definitely going soft already.

Mika positions himself in the doorway between the living room and kitchen and folds his arms across his chest in a perfect mime of a full-grown, dangerous *bratva* member. A stab of guilt pierces my shield of indifference toward the boy.

Am I really offering him no better than the life I was thrust into? Danger and darkness? Violence and mistrust?

Alessia sees the innocence in him still. How did I miss it?

I guess it's not something I look for.

I jog up the steps and collect the coffee and fast food. By the time I make it back downstairs, I find Alessia's engaged the boy in conversation. He's slicing an apple with his pocket knife and he offers her a slice.

Charming little princess. Her beauty probably gets her

everything. Beauty and a natural sweetness. She's untainted. Privileged, yes. But I wouldn't say spoiled. She's probably had the world wrapped around that little finger of hers from the beginning of her short, semi-charmed life, so she expects the best of people.

And they probably give it to her. Especially those who know about her diabetes.

Feeling inclined to give her a break, I set the food in front of her and let her use her own hands for a change.

The grateful look she shoots me makes my moment of weakness worth it.

I pull out a chair beside her and wave Mika into the other one.

Here we all are, one big happy family. I check her blood sugar to see if she requires insulin, even though she tells me checking once in the morning and once in the evening should be sufficient. She's right—she's okay.

"What's your favorite American food?" Alessia quizzes Mika.

He takes a huge bite of his double cheeseburger. "Piz-za," he says with his mouth full.

She nods sagely. "Pizza is pretty awesome. I am crazy about french fries, though." She dips one in ketchup and puts it in her mouth, rolling her eyes back like it's a bite of ambrosia.

Mika snorts, but the way his lips turn up tells me he's as fascinated by her as I am. Who wouldn't be?

I sit and watch her at work, coaxing Mika out of his surly shell as she devours the food I bought her, then sits back and sips the coffee. Every now and then, she darts a glance at me under her lashes.

When they finish, Mika gets up and leaves, and I reach to untie Alessia. And that's when everything goes sideways.

~

Alessia

I GRIP Mika's pocket knife in my sweaty palm.

Can I do it?

I have to.

If I don't get free now, I will end up on a plane to Russia, and my chances of escape or being found go way, way down.

Vlad bends over me, untying the knots that bind me to the chair. The moment he's done, I have to make my move. This is my best chance. I'll be untied, with only Vlad to overpower. I heard Mika step into the restroom, so he won't have to witness my act of violence. And if I do it right—a big if, considering I have zero practice at stabbing people—Vlad will live to take care of the boy.

Because I couldn't live with the guilt of orphaning him once more.

Really, if I were ruthless like one of my brothers, I'd go for his jugular. Stab to kill.

But I can't do it.

I'm queasy just thinking about breaking his skin.

He finishes untying me and grips my upper arms to lift me from the chair.

This is my chance.

With a swift upward motion, I bury the short blade in his gut.

He shouts something in Russian and jerks back, causing me to lose my grip before I get the knife all the way in.

I dart past him—at least I try to dart past him. He puts his body between me and the doorway, his hands gripping the handle of the knife. Blood seeps out, staining his t-shirt.

My eyes fill with tears at the sight of the wound, but I try again, lunging forward to get past him.

But a ferocious snarl in Russian stops me.

No, it's not the snarl, it's the gun.

It's the expression.

Young Mika stands behind Vlad, his face pale and tortured, a pistol wobbling in his shaking hands.

"Nyet!" Vlad yanks the knife out of his ribs and tosses it on the floor, then turns and grabs the gun.

I don't speak Russian, but it's easy to tell that whatever he's yelling at Mika isn't kind. It's a tongue-lashing of great magnitude. While he yells, he empties the pistol of its magazine and shoves it in the back of his waistband. All the while, he's bleeding profusely.

I feel like I'm going to puke.

Vlad continues scolding Mika. I'm not sure whether it's over allowing me to get ahold of the pocket knife or pointing a gun at me, but the boy's ears turn red and his jaw shifts right and left, chin wobbling slightly.

I'm actually feeling sorry for him, even though he might have just killed me.

Even though my chances of escape just diminished to zero.

The boy appears to attempt to defend himself, gesturing at me as he mumbles in Russian, but Vlad cuts him off with several more sharp words.

I can't move from where I'm standing. There's nowhere to go, anyway. I'm shaking all over, although I'm not sure if I'm more upset about what I did to Vlad, Mika's humiliation or what's about to happen to me.

When the boy shoves his hands in his pockets and looks away, blinking rapidly, Vlad finally relents. His voice gets quieter. More coaxing. He touches the boy on the shoulder, and says something else in softer tones. Ruffles the boy's hair.

Mika turns and escapes the way I wanted to.

When Vlad swivels back to face me, my stomach drops.

"Vlad," I whisper.

I don't know what I want to say. *I'm sorry? Don't hurt me? I wasn't trying to kill you?* Or maybe just *Please don't die.*

I don't know why I care, but it seems I do.

I blink furiously, but my eyes still fill with tears.

Vlad gives a short shake of his head as he takes a step closer to me. "Save the tears for your punishment, *printsessa.* I will live."

I let out a sound—half laugh, half sob and he throws me over his shoulder even though I should probably be the one carrying him at this point.

He moves slower than usual, but he gets me upstairs

and drops me on the bed, then rips off the t-shirt he put on me.

"Vlad," I croak again.

I push myself up on my elbows, breath coming fast, nipples puckered even though this isn't sex. What's he going to do to me?

He re-ties my hands in front of me, his movements deft and sure. Then he grabs my calves and tugs me off the end of the bed, flipping me over so my feet land on the ground, but my torso's flat on the bed.

Yeah, ass out.

Another spanking.

It's so out of proportion to what I just did to him that I want to laugh.

He tugs my panties down to my thighs and slaps my ass right and left a few times.

I welcome the sensation. If this is the worst he's going to give, I'm happy to take it. I just think he might need to get himself to a hospital in the meantime.

He pushes one hand into my lower back to hold me still and spanks hard. It's already sexual—everything about the punishment is sexual—my nudity, being tied up, being slapped so close to my pussy. But when he slides his thumb between my ass cheeks and pushes it against my asshole, my sexual response goes into hyperdrive.

Something seizes and lifts in my low belly, my pussy gushes, dripping onto my thighs. The sounds that come from my mouth sound distinctly like sex moans.

Vlad continues spanking my ass right and left a dozen or so times, jostling my hips and the contact of his thumb remains. He doesn't actually penetrate me, but it's always there, at my *most* intimate place.

And then he abruptly stops.

"Don't. Move," he growls.

That's an impossible order. Because, you see, my body's about to explode. Heat twists and arcs through me, pulsing in my core. Even though he released me, I'm intensely aware of my asshole. My pussy. The neediness coursing through me.

I turn my head and watch as he goes into the bathroom and strips off his bloody shirt, examining the wound in the mirror.

I shouldn't be turned on at a moment like this.

It's like all the fear just morphed into something dark and sexual. My ass is hot and stinging. Still bared to him.

He's manly to the Nth degree. He just took a knife wound without even a grimace. He pulled it out and tossed it on the floor like I'd scratched him with my fingernail. And the only anger he showed was toward Mika!

I shift and twitch my inner thighs together, trying to get relief.

"You stay in the position I put you," Vlad snaps from the bathroom, his accent thick. "If you move, I will spank you so hard you'll feel it all the way to Russia."

It's ridiculous. I'm now certain he's not going to hurt me. If this is the worst I get for trying to kill him, I'm not afraid. His biggest cruelty is leaving me here in this humiliating position, completely turned on and at his mercy.

Maybe I actually want that spanking.

I tug my elbows into my chest and shift to get my bound hands between my legs. I seriously need relief.

It's torture to not be able to turn my hands, angle my fingers where I want them, but I rub myself over my bound fists, getting friction on my clit.

From the bathroom I hear a sharp intake of breath.

~

Vlad

TY CHE, blyat.

I drop the bottle of superglue on the counter, transfixed by what I see on the bed.

My beautiful hostage is where I left her. *Masturbating.*

My dick lurches, lust rockets through me. I force myself to move slowly, to draw in a breath through my nostrils—exhale slowly through my mouth—as I walk up behind her.

"What did I tell you about moving?" My voice doesn't sound like my own. It's deep and rough. I slip my arm around her waist to pick up her hips and tug her arms back out, straightening them over her head.

I palm her pussy and lean over to speak in her ear. "Did I make you ache between your legs, Alessia?"

Her pussy's dripping wet, the folds swollen and welcoming. Without intention, one of my fingers sinks into her wet heat.

She moans, undulating her hips to take me deeper.

"Do you think you deserve pleasure after what you did to me?"

A tiny whimper comes from her. Her face is pressed

straight down into the mattress so I can't see her expression, but I nip her ear, caress her folds.

My cock strains

"Apologize," I demand.

"I'm sorry," she says immediately.

Poor pet. I believe she is sorry. The horror on her face the moment she knifed me said everything. She doesn't know violence. Didn't want to perpetrate it. And that makes me admire the fuck out of her attempt. She's brave. Strong for someone with a physical weakness. Stronger than I am, probably.

I slide a finger inside her again. She's tight but I work a second one in.

She humps the bed.

"Beg me, *zaika*. Beg me and I'll help you come," I challenge. Her scent fills my nostrils, sweet like honey cakes.

"No," she groans into the bed.

I still my fingers. "No?"

She shakes her head, rubbing her face over the coverlet.

Well, I'm not the dick who goes on when he's told no. Even if her *body* begs without pride. I remove my hand from her wet cunt and straighten up.

And then, maybe because I'm pissed, maybe just because I still want to give her what she needs, I start spanking her again.

Hard.

She arches her back, tipping up her ass for it, parting her legs.

I should make her suffer. Endure the sexual frustration

I'm experiencing. But I don't have it in me to torture her. I spank her hard and steady for a dozen strokes, then spank her pussy. Once.

Twice.

On the third time, she cries out and orgasms, her buttocks squeezing together, legs losing their footing as her toes point straight out.

If I weren't in so much pain myself, I'd smile because I am fucking proud of myself for being the man who gets her off, even when she claims she doesn't want it. But my testosterone rages, power and urgency ripping through me. I tear her lowered panties off her legs, then fist my fingers in her hair and use it to lift her head as I lean back over her. "Did I say you could come, Alessia?"

Her face is beautifully flushed, eyes unfocused and glassy. It takes her a moment to process my words, to find my face with her gaze. "No," she whispers with those pouty lips.

"No. *Nyet*. I didn't." I show her the panties. "You just lost your panty privileges, too." I drop them and reach back and slap her ass again. "Soon this pussy will belong to me. I'm the only one who gets to touch it, unless I give you permission to touch yourself. Your orgasms belong to me and me alone. If you want to come, you'll learn to beg, on your knees with my cock down your throat. Is that clear?"

I've gone way too far, but I can't seem to dial it back. My lust and frustration mingle into a potent fury.

Her throat works for a moment, then she spits out, "Fuck you."

My lips stretch into a feral grin. "Gladly, *printsessa*. I'll keep you up all night fucking."

She pales and some of my senses return. I loosen my grip on her hair, rub away the sting on her scalp.

"Next time you come without permission, you're going to feel my belt across that lovely ass," I warn.

I release her completely and she hides her face between her arms with a sob.

I straighten and look down at what a fucking perfect picture she makes on my bed. I rub her reddened ass, not sure why she brings out such tenderness in me. Maybe it's not tenderness but the need to show my ownership, prove my control.

Either way, I stroke her heated flesh in slow circles until she relaxes. Then I lift her fully onto the bed and pull the corner of the comforter up over her naked body.

lessia

I work to stop the trembling in my limbs as we board the plane. I had a plan—my last hope—to alert anyone and everyone I see that I'm a prisoner.

But there's no one. It's dark out, we're on a private flight and clearly every man here works for Vlad.

There's no one to scream to, no one to help me.

Vlad has an iron grip on my arm and he hustles me quickly onto the craft and pushes me into a seat. I notice he's favoring his hurt side a bit, which serves him right.

I can't really figure out how one Russian and a twelve-year-old kid can avoid the wide, wide net of the Tacone crime family.

How this can actually be happening. Me, going to Russia to supposedly marry the enemy.

"You're shaking," Vlad observes as he ties me to the seat.

"I don't want to go to Russia."

"Too bad," he answers immediately. "You're going."

"And you're a dick," I mutter. It's childish, but what else can I do? Calling him names is my only option when I'm tied to a seat on a private jet, surrounded by danger-ous-looking men.

Without my panties.

Yeah, he put my dress back on, but refused to let me wear panties. Said I'm still on restriction.

I know, big deal. I have far bigger problems than the fact that I'm bare-beaver under my dress, but it's screwing with my head.

Making me hot and horny and vulnerable. Making me think way too much about the spankings he gave me today.

The orgasms.

Vlad is everything dark, dirty and dominant I never dreamed about but must've always wanted, because he turns me inside out. Every interaction with him I come away changed.

He crouches beside me and tests my blood sugar. Normally, with a controlled diet and regular shots, I only check it once in the morning and once in the evening.

But he was right to check. The adrenaline that's making me shake made my blood sugar go haywire. He fills a needle with insulin like he's been doing this all his life.

I flinch when he goes to lift my dress. I have no panties on and Mika is sitting a few feet away. He stops and shifts to inject my upper arm instead.

This is part of why he turns me inside out. He's a first class asshole, for sure. A criminal who is taking me from everything I've ever known and loved. Holding me ransom. No, not ransom, he says he's keeping me. But for all that, he's also thoughtful. Aware of my reactions and needs. He may growl and threaten. He may talk a mean game, but he made a special trip to get the coffee I like. And he stopped when I said no.

I had to—there was no way I was going to beg.

No way in hell.

Which doesn't mean my body didn't completely revolt when he stopped. I'd been two breaths away from an orgasm.

And I can't believe I came anyway. Just from him spanking me.

That's what I mean about turning me inside out. I've never had a guy smack my ass before. I didn't know how much it turned me on. Didn't know about the desire that would steam, sizzle and bubble out of me like lava overflowing the side of a volcano.

Vlad rubs the injection site when he's done, then sits beside me for takeoff.

Across the aisle, Mika appears pale, his big brown eyes haunted. He grips the arms of his chair.

I lift my chin in his direction. "Is he afraid of flying?"

Vlad produces an orange from his bag and starts to peel it as he considers him. "I don't know," he murmurs. "Maybe Russia holds bad memories for him."

"Worse than America?" I ask drily. The poor kid was abandoned by his own mother here.

Vlad feeds me a section of orange. "Yes."

There's so much in that one word. Somehow I hear a lifetime of pain, both for Vlad and Mika. Or maybe that's just my imagination running wild.

"Could be he's worried about his future there," Vlad muses.

I tense slightly, worried too. "You'll keep him, right? Take care of him."

Something in the boy's posture tells me he might be eavesdropping. His shoulders stiffen and he goes perfectly still.

Vlad takes a moment to answer, which makes it all the worse. "If I survive this, yes."

"Survive what?" My voice is sharp. The urgency of securing that boy's future feels overwhelming.

He tries to feed me another section of orange, but I turn my face away. "Your attempts at escape."

I snort because we both know how pathetic my assault on him really was. And there's no way in hell he's afraid of me actually killing him.

He shrugs. "Your brothers," he amends.

A wash of cold runs over my skin, because he's right to fear them. They will kill him if they catch him. I have no doubt.

I look away, out the window of the plane at the Vegas lights glittering below. My brothers are down there right now. Looking for me. Pulling every string they have to try to find me.

And I'm right here. So close but out of reach.

Soon I'll be too far from their influence. Soon I'll be in a country where I don't speak the language and don't have a single friend.

I look over at Mika.

Maybe he feels the same way, minus the language barrier.

Vlad feeds me another bite of orange, then bends down and fishes another orange out of his leather satchel. "Mika," he calls out.

The boy turns and Vlad holds the orange up.

Mika shakes his head.

"Eat it," Vlad says firmly and tosses it to the boy who catches it with one hand. "You need your vitamins."

A smile flickers around the corner of his mouth before it quickly disappears again. He bends his head over the orange and peels it and both Vlad and I sit back in satisfaction.

When we reach altitude, Vlad unties me and shows me how the seat converts to a fully reclined bed. I go over and help Mika with his while Vlad produces pillows and blankets.

"You need anything? A snack? Something to drink?" Vlad asks.

"Are you our flight attendant?" I shouldn't tease when he's being nice.

He doesn't seem to mind. He smacks my ass lightly. "Shut up and sleep. Be good or I'll tie you to the bed."

"Aren't you going to sleep?" I ask. He hasn't converted a bed for himself yet.

He shrugs.

I wait for more of an answer but it doesn't come.

Okay, so the guy doesn't sleep.

Probably smart considering I tried to kill him today.

I sit on the edge of the bed. I'm exhausted but not

sleepy. Too much adrenaline. Too much worry. "What is there to drink?" I ask idly.

Vlad looks over from the leather captain's chair beside my bed. "What do you want?" He stands up, his movements lithe and graceful, like a panther. I stand and trail behind, happy to walk on my own two feet for a change. To be untied and free to move around.

In the tiny galley kitchen, there's a refrigerator stocked with all kinds of upscale drinks.

Vlad opens it and pulls out a bottle of Chardonnay. "You drink wine?"

It shouldn't make my heart flutter. We're not on a date.

Wine sounds so good right now, but I don't think my kidneys can take it.

"Seltzer water," I say.

He pours the water and hands me my glass then opens a drawer and produces a wine key. After he opens the bottle and pours himself a glass, he eyes me and pockets the wine key.

"Think I'm going to use that on you?"

Cristo. Am I flirting?

"I know you're thinking about it." His tone is light, like people around him often consider killing him and it doesn't faze him in the slightest.

I turn to slide past him, out of the tiny kitchen, but he shifts to block me from leaving. Pushes me up against the wall. His ribs pin my chest, one of his thighs presses between my legs. He holds his wine glass beside my ear and tips his head down to mine.

I gasp, my pulse picking up speed, heat flooding my body.

"You should know," he says, accent thick, "I'm having a hard time keeping my hands off you. Knowing your panties are in my pocket."

Some tiny whimper escapes my lips. "M-maybe you should give them back to me, then," I say. My voice sounds breathy and thin.

His erection swells against my belly. I unintentionally grind down on his thigh and the contact gets me wet.

"Tomorrow," he promises. "If you show me you can be a good girl on this flight. Then I won't have to keep you tied up any more."

I eyeball him. "How about if you don't keep me at all?"

He eases back, which comes as both a disappointment and relief. "Sorry, *printsessa*. Freedom isn't in the cards for you. You're mine now."

My nose burns and I draw a breath to hide the rush of tears threatening, but my eyes flood before I can look away.

Vlad's brows drop and he cups my face gently. Strokes my cheek with his thumb. "Not forever, *zaika*."

"How long?" I choke out.

He stares at me and I have the distinct feeling he's making this up as he goes along. There is no plan. It's both heartening and frightening at once. On the bright side, it means he's flexible. Changeable. I can influence him.

Maybe change my future.

"Until I grow tired of you," he says and drops his hand away. Steps back so I can pass.

As I walk in front of him, I'm acutely aware of every step. The wetness between my legs. The fact that his gaze is probably glued to my ass. I walk to the bank of chairs in front of my bed and sit down in the one by the window.

Vlad hangs back, gripping the bottle of wine in one hand and his glass in the other as he trails behind, watching me with hooded eyes.

I nudge the chair beside me. "Aren't you going to sit?"

I failed to get myself free before we left for Russia. Now my best shot is Vlad. Make nice. Endear myself to him. Beg for my freedom.

He's already conceded that I'll get it eventually.

It's my job to make sure that happens sooner than later.

Vlad

SHE'S DANGEROUS.

I know what she's up to. She's trying to wrap me around that pretty little finger of hers.

It's what she excels at.

I know this trap. It's the one all women work. They use their beauty, their sex appeal. They weave a web to ensnare you and then your balls are in a vise.

That's how Mika's mother got herself to America. How my mother ingratiated herself to Victor. How Sabina nearly got me killed.

And yet it's impossible for me to refuse. I'm already addicted to being near her, and all the more if she's playing nice.

I sit beside her and watch her drain her seltzer. I

could've sworn she wanted wine, but maybe she can't with the diabetes. I go and get the seltzer bottle and refill her glass and she murmurs her thanks and takes one more sip.

I watch her, fascinated as always by her beauty. Her poise.

She looks out the window, although there's nothing to see but inky blackness. "Where are we going again? Volgograd?"

"Yes." I don't elaborate. It entertains me to watch her work.

"Is it a big city?"

"Small city. One million people. Good place to live."

"Tell me about it."

There it is. A simple command. One I should resist, just to shut her down, but I can't. Not when she fixes those big brown eyes on me and leans slightly forward, lips parted, waiting.

I sip my wine. "Volgograd was formerly Stalingrad. Before that, Tsaritsyn. It's in southwest Russia on the banks of the Volga river. It's beautiful in summer. You will like it." It's stupid. I don't know why I think I have to sell it to her, but I find I want very much for her to like my city.

She looks away, the reminder that it will be her home probably stings.

"You have room for Mika there?"

There she goes with her concern for Mika again. If she's asking, she must think I have a small place, like the one in Vegas. It amuses me to think she might be surprised by my estate.

"Yes, Alessia," I say mildly. "There is plenty of room."

79

Her lips form a shape, like she's going to speak, then changes her mind. She tries again. "What...will I do there?"

I consider. "What did you do in Chicago?"

The light is dim, but I think she blushes. "My ma had surgery a few months ago, so I've been helping her out since I graduated in December."

I can't stop the smile. "You don't have to make an excuse to me for not working. I knew you were a kept princess. It will be no different in my house. Your brothers will supply the money to keep you in the style you've grown accustomed to."

Pain flickers over her face, but she hides it quickly. Looks away.

It shouldn't bother me. When you take a woman as tribute, you can't expect her to kneel at your feet and thank you for it.

When she turns back, her jaw is set, eyes challenging. "I need the Rosetta Stone for Russian."

I nearly choke on my wine. "You wish to learn Russian?"

She nods, determination emanating from her.

It's a wise choice. If she can speak the language, she will not be so helpless in Russia. It would be easier for her to escape or get help. But it's clearly a long game, and not an easy one. I admire the hell out of her for even considering it.

"Of course you can have it. You will have everything you need, *zaika*."

"Everything but my freedom?"

"*Da.*"

Her chin wobbles slightly, but she recovers, stares out the black windows.

"What did you study in college, Alessia?" Now I'm the one making conversation.

She turns back to me. "Early childhood education."

I arch my brows, surprised. I expected something inane like art history, or English literature. Some liberal arts degree with little application.

"You wish to teach?"

"Yes. I love children."

Of course she does. I look over at Mika, now asleep on his bed. No wonder she takes such an interest in him.

Knowing she has this humanitarian side, this reverence for children, stirs something in my chest.

"You want children?" Suddenly the image of her pregnant with my child floods my imagination. Draws out some primitive caveman protectiveness. I never wanted children, but the idea of knocking her up, of creating a family with her flips my world on its head.

But she flinches at my words and looks away. "I can't."

My disappointment is as ridiculous as the idea of having children with her was to begin with. But maybe I'm just feeling her pain. She's clearly deeply wounded by this.

"Why not?"

She doesn't answer.

"The diabetes?"

A tiny nod, but she's still looking away.

Oh, Alessia.

Surely people with diabetes have children. I make a note to research it, but a chill creeps over my skin. Alessia must have had the best doctors money can buy. If she believes she can't have children, it's with good reason.

I shouldn't feel pain over it.

It's just as well considering our marriage won't be a long-term one.

"I'm sorry," I mutter and she darts a glance my way. The vulnerability I glimpse on her face tears me up.

Alessia

DAMN VLAD. My eyes get hot and watery under his sympathetic gaze, and I have to look away again.

I wish he weren't so damn observant.

I haven't told anyone about the stage 3 kidney failure. Not any of my brothers, especially not my mother. So I haven't had to face this moment before, of revealing my sharpest disappointment in life.

Desperately needing to change the subject, I turn back to him and draw a breath. "What about you, Vlad? What is your job in Russia?"

"I am *derzhatel obschaka*. Bookkeeper for the *bratva*. I'm the money guy. I move money, launder money. Hide money. I had reached out to your brother not to cause problem, but to offer solution. Clean his money, too. But then my mother died in Moscow. I had to fly back to Russia, and Ivan, my idiot compatriot decided killing your family was a better option."

I blink at him, surprised at this information. I don't

want to find Vlad so likeable. Knowing he's not a drug dealer or sex trafficker or hitman, but more of a white collar thug, doesn't hurt his case. Knowing he has a mother—had a mother—makes him all the more real. Normal. Human.

"I'm sorry for your loss," I say.

Something fierce and raw appears on his face. Unexpressed grief. I get the feeling he hasn't been offered condolences. Or the loss is still too fresh. Or there are unresolved issues there. He drops his head and lets it hang. "My mother—*da*. I still don't believe she's gone. It's strange to go back and know she won't be there."

I reach out and touch his arm. He looks up, shocked. Like I branded him.

But his lips twist into a bitter line. "Don't feel sorry for me. I shouldn't miss her. She was a manipulative bitch, like every woman in my life."

I remove my hand, recoiling. Because I sense he somehow lumps me into that category, too.

I know I'm right when he narrows his eyes at me. "You can stop your game of trying to win my sympathies. Lie down on your bed. Go to sleep. Tomorrow is your wedding day."

My stomach lurches and I'm suddenly nauseous. I surge to my feet and square my shoulders, throwing the rest of my water back in my throat. "Where's my toothbrush?" I demand like the spoiled brat he seems to think I am.

I fully expect him to tell me to go fuck myself, but he reaches in his satchel and produces it—the toothbrush and travel toothpaste in a small ziplock bag. Still taking care of me.

I shouldn't like it. Shouldn't want any sort of attention from the man who's captured me and wants to force me to marry him.

I grab the bag out of his hand and march away to the bathroom, working hard to steady my breath and my nerves.

He won't win this game. Sooner or later I will escape. My brothers will find me.

And he'll be the one on his knees begging for mercy.

 *lessia*

WE LAND the following afternoon after a sixteen hour flight. I spent the morning playing cards with Mika and ignoring Vlad.

I'm on edge as we get off the plane and a swarm of tattooed men in suits and guns flank us and lead us to a limo.

If Vlad seemed like a one-man show back in the U.S., it's clear he's plenty connected on his home turf. I look out the tinted window, my hands clammy and my stomach in knots.

"It's normal for a bride to be nervous on her wedding day," Vlad observes and I shoot him my best death stare.

"Go fuck yourself."

Mika goes still, head bent over his tablet, as always, but clearly listening. Is he worried for my well-being now that we've made friends? I wonder if I can't convince him to help me somehow.

Then again, I'm not sure I'm willing to put him in the position of betraying the only parent figure he has in the world right now.

Vlad just chuckles, though. He doesn't seem to have a temper; at least not with me.

The limo pulls up in front of a church and the stone sitting in my stomach sinks even lower. We are actually doing this.

"You think you're going to get a priest to perform a wedding to a bride in a pink halter dress?" I ask. I'm so sick of this dress right now, I'd like to put it through a shredder. And Vlad hasn't given me my freaking panties back, either.

Vlad smirks. "I have a white dress for you. And a woman to help you dress. All you have to do is walk down the aisle."

I narrow my eyes. "I hate you."

"As it should be between husband and wife." He climbs out of the car and offers me a hand. I shake my head, but don't bother commenting on his piss-poor view of love, women or marriage. My dress rides up as I scoot out and his blue eyes darken, following the hem up my thigh. I shake off his hand and yank the dress down.

The church is empty. At least I won't be getting married in front of a crowd of people I don't know. Vlad deposits me in a small room where an old lady waits. She bustles over to me, speaking in Russian.

"Five minutes," Vlad tells me, then says something to the old woman in Russian. As he leaves, he points a threatening finger at me. "Try to escape and she'll be punished for it." He tips his head at the old woman.

My mouth drops open, heart beating faster.

It's a bluff, I tell myself as he shuts the door. He wouldn't hurt an old woman any more than he would hurt me. Or Mika. It's just that he has my number now. He's figured out I have compassion for the people around me and he's manipulating me with it.

Still, I'm reluctant to call his bluff. I definitely don't want an old woman facing his wrath.

The woman wears a dour expression and chatters at me in Russian, holding up a white bustier and panties and pushing me into the restroom.

Deducing she wants me to put on my undergarments in private, I go into the stall and shuck the halter dress. I showered in the tiny jet bathroom this morning, but it feels glorious to put on clean underclothing. The bustier and panties fit perfectly. How did Vlad know? He didn't even have a bra to go off of.

I come out of the bathroom. The old woman holds up a wedding dress. It's not bad as far as wedding dresses go. Definitely could be worse. It's strapless with a simple satin bodice. A satin band trims the top and makes a flat bow in the back. The dress is fitted through the waist and hips and flares out at the ankles, the hem falling higher in front than in back.

My elderly attendant thrusts a cascading bouquet of pale pink roses in my hands, then squats down at my feet, arranging several shoeboxes beside her. She says something in Russian and holds up a pair of silver strappy sandals.

I wrinkle my nose. "I don't love them, if that's what you're asking."

She bobs her head and says something else, unboxing a simple pair of white satin pumps.

I look at the third box. "What else do you have there?"

She opens it. Strappy white satin sandals.

I point to the pumps. "Probably those. Let's try them."

She gets the gist and helps me into the shoes. They're fine. Nothing special but they fit. As soon as they're on, she hustles me out the door to the chapel.

The knot in my stomach moves up to my solar plexus, making it hard to breathe. I'm sweaty and freezing at once. Just a few days ago I was at my brothers' double wedding lamenting I'd never have a love match like them. Even so I never dreamed my wedding would be like this. That I would be a captive bride in a foreign country.

This doesn't matter. It isn't real.

So I keep telling myself, but the sentimental part of me doesn't believe it. This is a wedding. A church wedding in front of God and a Russian Orthodox priest, who can't be that different from a Catholic priest.

There's no one playing *Here Comes the Bride* for me to walk down the aisle. There's no music at all. No guests, either, unless you count Mika and Vlad's horde of security guys.

"What, no tux?" I ask when he meets me at the rear of the church. He ignores me, taking my elbow instead of offering his. "Where's my headpiece? Seriously, I'm not getting married without a tiara. I thought I was your *printsessa* or whatever."

Vlad's lips twitch, but he doesn't look at me. "You

don't need tiara, you already have shiny halo." His accent's grown thicker since we arrived in Russia.

I snort.

I can't believe I'm walking down the aisle joking with my captor-slash-groom.

He stops in front of the priest, who waves the sign of the cross in front of us and chants in Russian.

There's some talking. Some more talking.

Then, apparently the vows. The priest looks at me.

"*Nyet,*" I say firmly.

The priest ignores me and goes on with the ceremony. At least I think that's what happens, but I can't be sure since the whole thing is in Russian.

As I stand there, trembling beside the man who is apparently marrying me, it strikes me just how screwed I really am. Not speaking the language, being in a foreign country is a huge disadvantage. Especially considering how connected Vlad appears to be.

The priest says something else and Vlad cups the back of my head and pulls me in for a quick peck on the lips. It all happens so fast I don't have a chance to fight it, and then it's over.

Fuck.

I'm married.

I hiccup on a sob.

Vlad scoops me into his arms and carries me out of the church as I drag in stuttered breaths. No tears come. Just crazy, heaving, erratic sobs. The kind that sound like a drowning woman gasping for air.

Mika walks along beside us, throwing worried glances up at me. Vlad walks swiftly to the limo. One of his men opens the door for him. Instead of dropping me inside, he sits on the seat and pivots his legs in, keeping me in his arms.

Mika slides in across from us, his brows down, head low.

Vlad barks something in Russian to the driver and the limo leaves as I continue to struggle with my breath. My fake groom holds me on his lap and strokes my bare arms with a light, feathery touch. His brows are down, same as Mika's, and he doesn't look at me.

I stare out the window at the landscape flying by, hiccupping, feeling the last bit of my hope draining away.

Vlad

I WANT to comfort my bride, but there's nothing to say. I'm the cause of her distress and what's done is done.

Still, it bothers me more than I care to admit to feel her shaking in my arms. To see her come undone.

"Will you let her go?" Mika mutters in Russian so quietly I barely hear it. He doesn't look at me when he asks.

"Yes. Eventually," I tell him, also in Russian.

He flicks his wary gaze at me and gives a single nod before looking out the window.

"I won't hurt her, and I won't force sex." It's a fucking awkward conversation to have with a twelve-year-old, but I feel like I have to tell him. I don't know what the kid's seen. His mother was a whore. I don't know how Aleksi or other johns treated her. Mika may be scarred from things that were done to her.

Worse, he might be deadened to the concept of consent, of how a woman should be treated. And I'm providing a shit example. So I need him to know this.

He doesn't answer, which is fine. I look at him until he glances back up at me.

"Never force a woman to have sex, Mika. It's wrong."

Uncertainty and pain flash in his eyes, and I'm glad I persisted. He is scarred.

"Do you agree?" I press.

He nods quickly. "*Da.*"

"Good." I release him from my gaze. I'm still stroking Alessia's arms. She's calmed down now, although I still detect a tremor in her limbs.

"You will like my place," I say in English, to both of them. "It's quite comfortable."

Neither one of them answer.

The limo pulls up at my sprawling country home on the bank of the Volga river at sunset. Rosy-hued clouds make a stunning backdrop for the stately mansion.

It's strange to be back. I've been away for thirteen months now. Banished to America because a conniving woman tricked me into her bed.

The servants know I'm coming. My housekeeper, Zoya —the servant who attended Alessia at the church—stands outside with her husband Yegor. My men line up outside to greet us, as well.

The driver opens my door and I lift Alessia out and

onto her feet and follow her out. Mika climbs out and takes it all in, nothing showing on his expression.

"It's nice," Alessia concedes, her gaze traveling over my enormous mansion and the gated grounds surrounding it. She points in the direction of the thicket of trees. "Is that the river?"

"*Da.*" I smile. She could so easily be a bitch right now. Decide to hate everything, show me only her ire. But she doesn't. Her first words are "it's nice."

She's nice.

So much sweeter than I imagined.

Guilt at stealing her from her life wars equally with the desire to keep her—permanently.

I reward her sweetness with the courtesy I didn't extend at the church. "Alessia, you already met Zoya, my housekeeper. She doesn't speak English, but she will see to all your needs. I will get you a translator until you learn from your Rosetta Stone."

Alessia sticks a hand out and Zoya reluctantly takes it and bows over it.

"Her husband, Yegor. He's the caretaker."

Yegor bows.

In Russian, I introduce Mika to my staff. I already advised them about my prisoner, but I forgot to mention my new ward.

Zoya glowers at him, like she's afraid he's going to mess up my house, but of course, she says nothing.

"Come, both of you. I'll give you a tour." I show them around the house. I've already given instructions to my staff to remove any access to phones or internet and my men will surround all exits to keep Alessia from leaving. This way, she can be free to move about the mansion.

"This will be your room, Mika." I open the door to one of the guest suites.

He goes over and sits on the bed, giving it a little bounce. Then he gazes at me, his blue-grey eyes searching. "For how long?"

I shrug. "We'll see." I'm not one to make plans or promises. I don't know how this thing with Alessia will play out. Or if I will even want to stay in Russia. I don't particularly even want to return to my former life here.

It was the wrong thing to say, though.

Alessia glares at me, lips tightening.

I frown back at her, but then sigh and try to make it right.

"You can stay here as long as you like, Mika. It's your home."

Apparently it still wasn't the right response because Alessia shakes her head at me.

I give her the "what?" gesture and she shakes it harder.

I toss Mika the remote to the television in his room. "Feel free. Or go explore. As you like." I wave my hand.

Outside the room, Alessia pulls me down the hall away from the room, but lays into me immediately. "Mika needs stability. You don't tell him he's *welcome* to stay. He's not a houseguest. You tell him he'll be with you, whether it's here or elsewhere. That he's yours and you're going to look after him." Now she digs in her heels and pulls us to a stop. "You are going to look after him, aren't you?"

I sigh.

This was not a commitment I was prepared to make.

The boy became my responsibility by default, not because I chose it.

"Listen, I wasn't looking to become a father. You know how unfit I am. I've involved the boy in serious crimes. Kept him from a proper education."

"He just needs someone to care about him. He's looking to bond. Until you make sure he knows you're committed, he's hardly got a shot at becoming a decent human being."

I curse in Russian and run my fingers through my hair. "Your opinion is noted," I grumble. "Now come on, bride. it's time to call in for your dowry."

Alessia

MY DOWRY.

"Are you calling my brother?" I ask as Vlad leads me into a master suite.

"Da." He retrieves a tablet from the leather satchel he always has with him.

"Which one?"

"I'm calling Junior. Is he not the head of the Family?"

I lift one shoulder. "Yes and no. Officially, yes. But Nico holds the financial power."

"Yes, Nico. He runs the Bellissimo."

Flutters fly in my belly. Just talking about my brothers makes them seem closer. More able to find me and rescue me. "Can I talk to them?"

"If you're good. I will put you on video so they can see you are well. But no funny business." He points a stern finger at me.

I look down at the wedding gown. They will see me on my wedding day. My eyes sting. Married to a criminal. That part was expected, I just thought it would be one of their choosing.

Vlad leans against a dresser and uses his phone, then powers up the tablet.

A moment later the tablet starts ringing. Vlad smirks as he slides his finger across the screen.

"Junior. Remember me?"

"Vladimir." I hear the darkness in Junior's voice. The threat.

"I have something of yours. Someone, actually."

Junior curses in Italian. In the background I hear my other brothers' voices.

"If anything happens to Alessia, I'll rip your spine out. Where is she?" Junior's voice booms from the tablet.

I scramble over to Vlad's side to see. I half expect him to keep me from it, but he doesn't, he lets me lean in beside him, filling the screen with my face.

Junior's face fills the screen on the other side, but I see parts of Nico and Stefano behind him.

"Alessia," Junior speaks quickly. "Tell me where you are." He says it in Italian—clever thinking.

"Volgograd!" I shout.

Stupid, stupid, stupid.

Vlad immediately rips the tablet away from me, holding it high in the air and ending the call.

"No," I sob as the tablet goes silent. "Wait—*please.* I'm sorry."

I suddenly care less about being found than I do about just seeing my family. Talking to them. Letting them know I'm okay. I saw the dark circles under Junior's eyes. The deeper lines. He should be on a honeymoon right now, not frantic over me.

"Now you lose privileges." Vlad takes a menacing step in my direction. His face is hard. I swear, he's more annoyed with me now than he was when I stabbed him.

"Let me talk to them. Please. Or just let me see them. Mute my side, I won't say a word."

"*Nyet.*"

"Please. No Italian. No funny business—I swear." Tears fall down my cheeks. I can't stop them. I'm suddenly so homesick. So alone.

The tablet rings again.

Vlad points at the bed. "Sit."

I sit where he tells me, giving him big begging puppy eyes. The white pumps drop from my feet.

Vlad answers the call. "You may have noticed your sister's bridal gown. Today we married. I am so pleased to make this alliance with American mafia," he says, like he's giving a toast at our reception. "You can count on me to treat her well so long as you wire me the funds to keep her in the style she's accustomed to."

I hear one of my brothers curse under his breath in Italian.

"Six million. One million for each of my men you killed, paid over twenty-four months. That's a quarter million a month. I will text you the routing and account numbers. First payment is due in four hours." He looks at his watch.

"We send it all now and Alessia comes home," Junior growls.

"*Nyet*. She's my bride. She stays with me. Twenty-four months. How she's treated depends on you."

Another Italian curse. Sounds like Stefano.

"Let us see her again." It's Nico's voice now. "We need to know you haven't harmed her."

Vlad glances over at me, then back at the screen. "You speak Italian, I end the call. How do you say it—*capiche*?"

"Understood," Stefano says.

I sit up straighter, wiping my eyes as Vlad sits beside me and holds the screen in front of us.

"What did you do to her?" Junior explodes, noting my tears.

I shake my head. "He didn't hurt me." I wipe the rest of the moisture from my eyes. "I'm just being a baby. It's good to see you guys."

"Lessie," Stefano says softly, with so much sympathy in his voice, I tear up again.

"I'm fine." I sniff. "Just homesick. Tell Ma I'm okay. And send the money. It goes to the boy Junior orphaned when he shot all the Russians."

Junior goes still.

Vlad takes the tablet and stands up. "*Da*. Send the money. You have four hours." He ends the video call and regards me. The planes of his face fall in harsh lines. He's irritated, maybe even angry, it's hard to tell. Even though he's been decent to me, I see the danger in him—coiled potential right there below the surface.

I grip the edge of the bed with both hands. Butterflies flit in my tummy.

Now you lose privileges.

Which ones? Clothing privileges? What will my punishment be? Will he strip me naked and tie me to the bed again? Spank me?

The memory of the last spanking he gave me, holding me in place with his thumb against my anus floods my mind.

My pussy clenches even as my palms sweat.

But "It's hard to stay angry with you," is all he says as he walks to the door. "There are clothes in the dresser. Basics. Tomorrow we can buy whatever you need." He shuts the door and I hear a key turn in the lock.

I run for it and try the handle. Bang on the wood. "Vlad!" I shout.

I don't know why I'm so panicky—I should be happy I'm not tied up. I'm just locked in a bedroom. And a very luxurious one at that. But I don't like it. Loneliness claws at my chest like desperation.

"Vlad!" I scream.

"Easy, *zaika*." The key scrapes in the lock again and the door opens a few inches. Vlad leans against the door-frame, his face close to mine. "You lost your freedom for tonight. You have to stay in the room. Tomorrow we can try again—if you're a good girl, I'll let you out."

My throat bobs, but I can't quite swallow. "Are you coming back?" I quaver.

It's pathetic. Am I really begging for his company?

Yes, I am.

I don't want to be alone tonight. I'm in a foreign country, thousands of miles from my big, noisy Italian family. With no hope of seeing them any time soon.

I'm desperate for human interaction of any kind. And I'm growing used to—if not fond of—his company, in particular.

His expression softens and he studies me for a moment.

I try to wipe the vulnerability from my face, but I doubt I'm successful.

"It's my room, *zaika*," he says mildly. "I'll be back."

It sounds more like a warning than a comfort, but I'm relieved anyway. When he closes the door, I sit down on the bed and indulge in a good cry.

Vlad

I SEND Zoya to Alessia with a tray of food and pace around the mansion. Mika is settled in his room, already eating from a tray. Good. Zoya will take good care of him. I had a feeling. She may look dour, but underneath the rough exterior is a soft heart.

Blyat, it nearly killed me to walk away when I could hear Alessia crying behind the door. I only left in the first place because I doubted she wanted me around. Because I didn't dare punish her by removing her clothes. Or smacking that beautiful ass of hers. Because seriously— another round of her coming from my punishment and I won't be able to hold back. I will hold her down and fuck her raw.

But then she asked if I was coming back—like she didn't want me to go.

Fuck.

Now I can't stay away. Leaving her alone is an impossibility.

I check my accounts and find the money has already been wired from Alessia's brothers. I expected them to comply, but seeing how quickly they responded satisfies me. It's good to know she is as cherished by them as she should be. They are taking no chances with her safety.

I make a round of the estate, making a mental list of updates and maintenance that need to be done, then go back to the room.

The tray of food is gone and Alessia's moving around in the bathroom. I hear the bathtub drain and a few minutes later she walks out wearing one of my t-shirts and a pair of the panties I had Zoya buy, along with other basic clothing items..

It would be night in the U.S. even though it's only mid-day here. She must be getting ready for bed.

My cock thickens. She smells fresh, like cucumbers and fruit.

She looks ripe enough to eat.

All afternoon long.

She stops when she sees me, breath catching. "We're not consummating the marriage."

"Eventually, *zaika,* you'll beg me for it."

She scoffs. "Keep telling yourself that." But her fingers tangle with one another like she's nervous.

"Come"—I pat the bed—"I need to check your blood sugar."

She advances, wariness in her step.

I test her blood sugar and it looks good. I'm half disappointed, half relieved I don't get to lift that t-shirt and see what she looks like in a different pair of panties when I administer her shot.

She yawns.

"You're ready for sleep? You should really wait until it's dark out. Reset your internal clock. Or so they say."

She walks to the windows and closes the shades. "There. It's dark."

I try and fail at withholding a smile. There's something so fresh and easy about her. She pushes but it's not bratty. Not bitchy. Apart from her meltdown after the call with her brothers, she's rolled with her abduction remarkably well.

She's one in a million, for sure.

I want to kiss her. The thought surprises me, because I'm not the kissing type. I'm more of the type to pound a woman from behind and never ask her name. But she has those full, shapely lips. I want to taste them. Savagely.

And slowly.

And every manner in between.

She pulls the covers back on the bed and climbs in.

I'm suddenly fuck-all tired myself. I haven't slept more than a few hours in days now, not wanting to let my guard down. But now that I'm in Russia, with *bratva* soldiers all around to guard my kingdom, I can sleep.

I get up and brush my teeth, then strip down to my boxer briefs.

Alessia watches from the bed, her eyes on the wound she gave me. I touch it. It's healing fine. Still tender, but not infected.

I climb in under the covers with her and listen to her breath go shallow. She's afraid of me, of course. Or maybe excited. A little of both, probably.

After five minutes of silence, she says, "You could touch my head if you wanted."

I smile and push myself up to my elbow. She's facing away from me, curled on her side. "You want me to massage your head again?"

"Yes?" she says in a small voice. It sounds like a question. Like she's not sure about what she's asking. Maybe she knows she shouldn't invite me to touch her.

"Say please. *Pozhaluysta*." I give the word in Russian.

"You have a thing about me begging, don't you?"

I burrow my fingers in her hair.

She makes a soft whimper in reply.

"*Pozhaluysta*," I direct her again.

"Mmm. Fine. *Pozhaluysta.*" Her pronunciation is not half bad.

I reward her with steady strokes. I find the sutures of her skull and rub gentle circles along them, fist my hand in her hair and pull from the roots.

She makes soft noises of contentment for a few minutes and then, judging by her slowing breathing, falls into slumber.

 *lessia*

I WAKE up at 10 p.m. Vlad was right; I should've waited for dark to go to sleep, but after the emotional drain of seeing my brothers and getting homesick, I didn't have it in me to stay up another minute.

He's asleep beside me. First time I've seen him sleep.

I study him. Examine the tattoos up close. They're crude and ugly, but he's beautiful. The need to touch him, to trace those defined muscles, feel his ripped abs is over-whelming.

I do want to have sex with him. I want to straddle his waist right now and see what it's like to feel him inside me.

But there's no way I'm letting him know that. He's taken everything else from me—I'm not going to hand over the one thing he lets me keep.

I get out of bed and search the room. I was in too much of a fog when I arrived, but now I look for any electronic —his phone, tablet—anything I could use to contact my brothers.

Of course, I find nothing.

He's thorough, my Russian. Smarter than he appears to be. But then, he'd have to be smart to be the money guy for the entire Russian *bratva*.

I go through his things, looking for clues about him, but there's nothing of a personal nature. No photos, so papers, not even an ID.

"Stop snooping, little bunny." Vlad's voice, thickened with sleep, comes from the bed.

I jump and turn around. It's on the tip of my tongue to apologize, but I'm not really sorry, so I save it.

"Are you hungry? Let me check your blood sugar."

I am getting shaky. "It's low," I tell him.

He curses and swoops out of bed, picking up the testing kit and coming at me.

He has a killer case of morning wood. At least I think it's a killer case. I wouldn't really know. I stare at the flagpole filling his boxer briefs.

"Beg for it, *zaika*, and it's yours," he rumbles as he bends over my finger.

"Go to hell, Vladimir."

His lips twitch, but he doesn't take his attention away from the syringe.

"Is that your real name?"

"*Da*." He lifts me by the waist to sit on his dresser, then hikes up the t-shirt I used as a nightshirt and injects my belly.

"What's your last name?"

"Putin." He's leaning over me, so close I can feel his heat.

"Very funny."

He drops his gaze down to my panties. "These are pretty."

My knees are open and before I can slap them closed, he runs one knuckle down my panty-clad slit.

My internal muscles seize in pleasure, but I squeeze my thighs together, shooing his hand away.

One corner of his lips lift, but he doesn't try anything else. "What are you hungry for?"

"Honestly? Pancakes. But they're too carb-y. So spinach and mushroom omelette."

"I'll get Zoya."

"Isn't she asleep now?"

He shrugs. "She works when I need her to."

"That's kind of an asshole thing to say."

"*Da.* I'm asshole. You should know this by now." He pulls a t-shirt over his head and steps into a pair of jeans. "Come." He holds his hand out to me.

I don't want to take it, but I also don't want to refuse— not when it seems he's offering me a chance to get out of the room.

I offer my hand and he leads me through his enormous mansion to a beautiful kitchen. Everything is contemporary and new. Sleek and European styled appliances and granite countertops.

I walk to the refrigerator and open it. There's a carton of eggs, which I grab.

I stiffen when I feel Vlad right behind me, but he

doesn't try anything. Just reaches past me and pulls out butter, cheese and milk and some kind of fresh greens—I don't recognize the leaves.

"Omelette."

"Yes, please."

Despite saying he was going to get Zoya up, he pulls a frying pan out and makes quick work of preparing and cooking two perfect cheese omelettes with greens.

When he serves it to me—complete with a smattering of sliced green onion on top—I sit at the barstool and wolf it down.

"You *were* hungry," he observes, sitting beside me and forking his own food. "Did you eat anything before you went to bed?"

"Not much," I admit. I'd been too overwrought emotionally to want to eat.

I carry my plate to the sink, rinse it off and put it in the dishwasher. "How long have you lived here?"

"I bought the place six years ago. But I've been in the U.S. for the last thirteen months."

"Yes, obviously. But why?"

"Why what?"

"Why would you leave this beautiful place to live in Chicago? I mean, you're obviously doing quite well for yourself here."

His brows draw together. Expression tightens. "I was ordered to leave. By Victor, the papa."

"The papa?"

"That's what we call the head of the *bratva*." He scrapes his fork on his plate, scooping up the last of the eggs.

There's something there. The energy in the room changed from relaxed to charged.

"Was it a punishment?" I ask.

He slides a glance at me, then shrugs. "In a way." He stands and walks to the sink. "Too many questions, *printsessa*."

"What else am I going to do? I'm wide awake at 10 p.m. with no one but you for company."

His gaze drops to my breasts, bare beneath the thin t-shirt and his expression turns feral. "I can think of a few things we could do."

"I'll bet." I'm doing my best to sound put off, but the truth is, my heart's racing. My nipples got hard. My pussy's tingling.

"Soon, *printsessa*—"

"I know, I'll beg. Keep dreaming, Russian." I saunter toward the door. "Are you going to show me around?" I admit, I put a little lilt in my voice. An invitation.

Vlad's gaze is hooded, his eyes on my bare legs. I should've put more clothing on before coming out of the bedroom. "Keep flirting, *zaika*, and it won't end well for you."

I cock a hip. "What's that supposed to mean?"

He adjusts his package, and I no longer require an answer. The tent in his jeans is impressive, to say the least. "My self-control is running out."

My cheeks grow warm. My panties dampen.

He walks toward me like a lion stalking his prey.

I smirk and take off running.

"*Blyat*," Vlad swears. He catches up five steps later,

banding an arm around my waist and lifting me from the ground.

"Vlad," I giggle, breathless.

"You must want my punishment," he growls in my ear. His breath is hot against my neck as he carries me toward the bedroom.

"No." I giggle, squirming in his arms.

It's one of those nos that definitely means *yes*.

I'm dying for his punishment.

And at the same time I know this is a bad idea. The wrong game to play. I shouldn't invite his touch. Give the wrong idea. Not when my intention was to refuse sex with him.

But it's like my body doesn't care. My flesh is on fire, craving his dominating touch.

And he gives it to me.

He carries me into his bedroom and uses one of his ties to bind my wrists to the headboard.

"No, wait," I pant, swishing my legs up and down over the expensive bedspread.

"Too late, *printsessa.* You ran. Now you have to be tied up." His normally pale blue eyes glitter dark as he stares hungrily at my body. He drops to his hands and knees over me and I catch my breath, my hips rocking up.

He palms both my thighs and pulls my knees apart. Lowering between my legs, he nips at my pussy, his teeth sliding over the silk gusset of the panties I found in the drawer here along with other clothes in my size.

"You choose your punishment." His voice is thick and deep. "My hand on your ass or my mouth on your pussy."

"Mouth." I barely get the word out. It's more like a squeak.

What I really want is both. All of it. The whole shebang. But mouth sounds positively delicious.

I'm rewarded with a leonine grin. He rips my panties down my legs and tosses them over his shoulder. Then he slides up between my legs with bald intent.

I shiver before he even touches me, and when he licks up my slit, my hips jack off the bed. He licks again. The strangled sound must be coming from me.

I'm so freaking sensitive—like every nerve is firing down there. He could just breathe on my pussy and I think I'd come.

I've been eaten out before, but it was nothing like this. That was a few swipes of the tongue to prepare me. This? This is like being zapped with a pleasure taser. It's too much, yet not enough. It's ecstasy with the pain of need mixed in.

Especially when Vlad begins to circle my clit with his tongue, to suck on it.

He screws a finger inside me and I writhe, ready to explode.

He backs off, removing his mouth and shoving my t-shirt up to expose my breasts. I think he's going to suck one of my nipples now, but instead, he reaches up and slaps my breast from the side.

I give a little mewl of alarm.

He slaps it again.

I moan.

He pinches my nipple as he rubs his lubricated fingers

up along my slit and back down again. I wriggle beneath him in pleasure, moan and croon and hum.

He slaps my breast. Now he moves up and sucks my nipple, teasing the taut bud with his teeth. Then he's back to working my clit with his tongue as he strokes my inner walls with two fingers deep inside me.

I choke. Cry out. Come.

Vlad doesn't stop the whole time I come, just strokes and sucks until I'm through grinding on his face, squeezing his fingers with the flutters of my release.

As soon as I finish, he rises up to stand on his knees and unbuttons his pants.

"No," I shake my head.

I know I'm a bitch, but I don't want to give him this. He stole me from my family. He doesn't deserve to consummate this unhappy marriage.

But he just smirks and pulls out his cock. I watch, breath rasping in short, panicked gulps as he fists his erection and jacks it with his hand.

Oh.

He's not going to rape me.

Relief becomes excitement as I watch his hand fly, the purpled head of his cock swollen and glistening with pre-cum.

It doesn't take him long until he spews, coating my belly with ribbons of his hot cum.

My head falls back on the pillow and I sag as the relaxation of my orgasm pours through me.

Vlad drops to his hands and lowers his head, kissing my fluttering belly. It's a soft, lingering kiss and it sets off another mini orgasm. "Soon, Alessia," he reminds me as I hold my breath, trying to hide it.

I don't want to admit he's right.

For orgasms like this, I probably will beg.

CHAPTER 10

 *lad*

ALESSIA SLEEPS A FEW HOURS MORE. I stay and work in the bedroom for a while, but eventually I head into my office.

I leave the door unlocked. I have men stationed at every door, inside and outside of the building. She's not going anywhere. And I don't want to see her upset again.

I push back the undercurrent of guilt that I've built this entire operation on. It started out as a way to punish the Tacones and line my pockets. But if I'm honest with myself, I have to admit it's turned into something else.

I would've said no to returning Alessia immediately for six million regardless. I am that big of a bastard. But keeping her here has become far more about my desire to have her in my house—in my bed—than it is about throwing my weight around with the American mafia.

I sit down at my desk and sort through the mail.

There's a stack of letters from Sabina. I pitch them in the garbage without opening them.

Conniving bitch.

I pop open my laptop and start moving money around to shell accounts. Dividing the Tacones' payment into smaller and smaller pieces until it disappears into the multitude of businesses I have set up.

Then I remember my promise to Alessia to set up an account for Mika and I work on that. When the boy appears in the doorway, rubbing his eyes, I call him in.

"Mika, come here." I beckon him over. "I want to show you something." I drag my cursor down a long list of accounts and show the tally of $95,000 at the bottom. "You know what this is?"

He shakes his head.

"This is your money."

He goes still.

I gesture toward my bedroom. "Money from the girl. For you."

He stiffens and takes a step backward. "I don't need it," he says quickly, and I realize he thinks I'm trying to keep him on board. To buy his complicity. And he wants no part of it. "Maybe you should just let her go."

A fresh wave of guilt rises, but I ignore it. I'd felt almost cheerful creating the accounts for him, putting the money away to ensure he's taken care of, no matter what happens to me. I want him to understand this is a good thing. Spawned by Alessia's compassion. "She insisted," I tell him. "Because her brother killed Aleksi, your guardian."

"Aleksi wasn't my guardian," Mika snarls.

I turn and give him my full attention. The boy's upset now.

"No?"

"He was the asshole who made my mother run away."

A sick feeling stirs in my belly. So he blames Aleksi for his mother's abandonment. He may be right. He may not. His mother might've just been a cunt who didn't care about her son. That's how it read to me, anyway. But I have a jaded view of mothers. And women in general.

But Aleksi probably was an asshole, to both Mika and his mother. I never liked the prick.

"Aleksi was a cock-sucking asshole, you're right," I agree mildly. "But Alessia feels responsible for you being left on your own after your cell was taken down. She demanded I use her money to provide for you. So here it is. If anything happens to me, you're the only person who can access these accounts."

He eyes me warily, like he doesn't quite believe it. "That's my money?" he asks.

"*Da*."

"Can I have it now?"

"No. Not unless you need it. Do you need something, Mika?"

His shoulders slump. "No."

I study him, trying to figure out what's going on inside that head of his. "I will give you a weekly allowance, so you have your own money to spend," I tell him and he brightens. "But only if you do a good job with your studies."

"What studies?"

"The studies Alessia is going to start you on." I'm

making it up as I go along, but it strikes me as a brilliant plan. Alessia is a teacher. She already cares about Mika. And she'll need something to do here—a purpose. I'll put her in charge of his education, and she'll settle into her life here.

They both will.

Something unfamiliar yet not unpleasant stirs in me at that thought.

The desire to make it happen—to create the environment where both of them might be content, even happy, sneaks into my agenda.

 ∾

Alessia

I WAKE UP BEFORE DAWN. I wasn't really sleeping—just snoozing. The restless, dream-filled sleep where you drift in and out of sleep and have trouble distinguishing when you're dreaming and when you're awake.

Like I'm lying in the bed, with Vlad massaging my head, and then we're in the kitchen making breakfast again. Only this time, he lifts me to the counter and holds my pelvis down while he licks me until I scream. And then we're in the bedroom with my brothers on the video screen, but he won't let me see. And I kick him, but it doesn't do any good because I'm barefooted. And he thinks it's amusing and then he pulls me over his lap like a child and spanks me for it.

And I get excited by the spanking and hump his lap, but he won't get me off because I refuse to beg.

I wake up horny and hangry. The omelette feels like days ago. I climb out of bed, legs shaky. Apparently orgasming and dreaming about Vlad burned a lot of calories. I would shower first, but I don't think I'll make it without eating something. I really need to keep some food by the bedside table for emergencies.

I pull on a pair of jeans I find in the dresser and stumble out in the direction of the kitchen. At least I think it's the right direction. It's hard to say—it was night and everything was dark.

I round a bend and run into Vlad and Mika coming down the hall toward me.

"Alessia?" Vlad walks swiftly to my side. "You're hungry, huh? Did you check your blood sugar?"

I shake my head, and the hallway swoops around me. "Hungry," I croak.

In a flash, Vlad swoops me up into his arms and carries me to the kitchen. "Get some juice from the refrigerator," he commands Mika, who stayed close.

A few moments later, a glass of juice is pressed to my lips and I drink, gratefully.

"Go get med kit from the bedroom," Vlad says, then switches to Russian, speaking quickly—like it was too much to explain the location of the kit in English.

Mika takes off at a run and returns just as fast. Vlad props me on a barstool and tests my blood and gives me a dose of glucagon. He peers into my eyes, his brows pinched tight.

"Too much sleeping and not enough eating," I say weakly. My schedule's off with the jetlag. It screwed up my blood sugar. I haven't eaten enough. I'm not sure. Avoiding situations like this is why my family wants me on a full-time insulin pump, an idea I detest. I've worked hard to never have an incident, so I'm pissed at myself. But then, I've never been kidnapped and brought to a foreign country against my will.

"I fucked up," Vlad says angrily, rubbing his forehead. "Should've been checking more often."

Of course it's not his responsibility, it's mine, but I go with it, anyway. "You can make it up to me by setting me free."

Vlad tests leaving me unsupported on the barstool, and when I don't fall off, he shouts something in Russian and walks to the refrigerator. Zoya bustles in, looking at no one as she whips out a frying pan and fires up the stove. Vlad hands her a metal bowl he's taken out of the fridge.

Butter sizzles and then the sweet smell of pancakes fills the kitchen.

My favorite breakfast, but one I almost never indulge in. I muster a smile. "I really shouldn't have pancakes."

"These are special, high-protein pancakes. Good for diabetics."

"Really? Wow. Thank you. I'm so happy."

He nods but still wears the frown between his brows.

"Relax. I'm feeling better. I'm not going to die yet."

Not this year, anyway.

I hope.

A few minutes later, a plate of pancakes and bacon slides in front of me and I nearly weep with pleasure.

"Thank you. Thank you. Thank you. How do you say thank you in Russian?"

"*Spasibo.*"

I shouldn't love the deep rumble of Vlad's voice so much.

"*Spasibo,*" I repeat, looking at Zoya.

She turns her head in my direction and inclines it, but doesn't quite meet my eye. She's not the most personable of servants, but clearly beggars can't be choosers. I'm going to have to make friends with her as quickly as possible if I want to get off this continent.

Mika and Vlad their own plates of pancakes and bacon and the three of us shovel food in our mouths in silence for a moment.

"When do I get my Rosetta Stone?"

Vlad's lips tip up slightly. As always, he appears slightly amused by my demands, rather than pissed. I guess I'm lucky I have a captor who seems taken with me. This situation could be a hundred times worse. A thousand, probably.

"You get it when you get it."

"I need Spotify, too. Or Apple music. Something to listen to." Now I'm just testing him. Really what I need is access to the internet.

Of course, he knows what I'm up to.

"Nice try. You give me a playlist, I'll download."

"Did my brothers send the money?"

"*Da.*"

"I want to go shopping. Aren't you supposed to be keeping me in the manner I'm accustomed to?"

Again, a hint of a smile on his face. "When you earn an outing, you'll get one."

Arousal heats between my legs when I consider how I might earn such a thing.

I'm guessing sex would get me a long way with Vlad.

Too bad I'm not willing to give it to him.

Although after last night, I'm not sure how much longer my resistance will take before it crumbles.

"When do my studies start?" Mika asks.

I snag a piece of bacon from Vlad's plate and pop it in my mouth. "What studies?"

"I thought you could tutor him," Vlad says, dropping the rest of his bacon onto my empty plate.

"What about school?" I ask.

"No school," Mika growls in a perfect imitation of Vlad.

I roll my eyes. "Why not? Don't you want to be around kids your own age?"

He shakes his head emphatically. "I want you to teach me."

"Will you?" Vlad forks a stack of pancakes.

My mind is already running ahead with what it would take to get him going—assessments in each subject, etc. "It would have to be in English, of course. He would need someone else to teach Russian reading and writing."

"I don't need Russian."

"I won't be able to assess that," I tell Vlad.

"I will assess and get other tutor if he needs it," Vlad offers.

Mika brightens.

"I will need access to download a curriculum."

"I'll get what you need," Vlad promises.

"Today?" I ask.

"Are we starting today?" Mika actually seems excited about the prospect. It occurs to me that he's had far too little adult interaction or supervision. He's ready to soak anything up, even tutoring in school subjects.

"Yes," I say, even though I don't know what I'm doing yet. The kid needs structure. I'm going to give it to him, starting today.

I look at the clock on the wall. "We will meet from 9 to 12 every day, Monday through Friday. You get weekends off to play."

Mika snorts at the word *play*.

"You'll have to learn to play. I know you had to grow up faster than you should've, but somewhere in there, there's still a kid who wants to play." I ruffle his hair and he ducks out of my reach. "Now go take a shower and comb your hair. I'll meet you…" I hesitate.

"You can study at dining room table." Vlad waves his hand toward the adjoining dining room with the long, beautiful cherry wood table.

"I'll meet you there at nine," I tell Mika firmly in my best school teacher voice.

He slides off his stool, leaving the plate on the table.

"Ah ah," I chide sharply. "Take that plate to the dishwasher and tell Zoya *spasibo*."

He obeys and Zoya seems pleased, glancing over at me with a bob of her head.

Vlad's phone rings. "Excuse me, *zaika*, I have business to attend to. If you need anything, Zoya will help you."

"Right, because I speak Russian so well," I snark at his

back as he walks out of the room speaking in terse Russian to his phone.

Vlad

I ANSWER to Victor all morning—taking his calls, dealing with his money, joining conference calls, but all I'm thinking about is the way Alessia looked orgasming last night.

The taste of her pussy.

The feel of her supple skin beneath my hands.

I want to spread those thighs wide again and make her scream. I want her in trouble with me—ass bared and spanked, hands tied.

I want her breathless and hot and ready.

But I'm not going to push. Time is on my side. Alessia's my prisoner, here for two years, maybe more. I know she's turned on by me. Her body responds. So it's just winning her mind now. Her heart. Bending her will.

And I have her right where I want her.

In my home.

My bed.

I'll learn what she likes, give it to her. Eventually, she'll let me in. She's already so unguarded. So unde-fended. She's kind and compassionate; she gives herself easily. Such a perfect creature, inside and out.

She almost makes me reevaluate how I view women.

Almost.

I finally beg off the phone with Victor in the afternoon and leave my office to find her. Make sure she's eaten lunch and see how it went with Mika.

I hear a screech from her at the front door and go running.

Blyat, no.

The door stands open and one of my soldiers is wrestling her back from it. I stride swiftly over. Alessia's cheeks are flushed with ire, eyes flashing. She stomps on my soldier's foot, elbows his ribs.

"Get your fucking hands off her," I shout in Russian with the menace of a thousand deaths. Another soldier hangs back, ready to jump in, but too afraid of me to make the wrong move.

He freezes and releases her slowly. "You said to keep her from—" She tries to dart past him, outside, but he blocks her way with his body.

"Yes, keep her inside. I didn't say you could fucking touch her. This is my bride. You don't ever fucking dishonor my bride, you understand me? She will be treated with the utmost respect. If I give you an order to limit her actions, you'd better fucking figure out how to accomplish it and still treat her like a fucking queen. Am I perfectly clear?"

"Yes, Vladimir." He and the other soldier both answer quickly, ducking their heads.

"Alessia, come." I beckon with my finger. I'm not going to manhandle her after she's just been assaulted.

She glares at me. "I want to go for a walk." She's dressed in a pair of jeans I had Zoya buy for her and a tight women's t-shirt. The kind that fits around the breasts and makes them look edible. She has a pair of sneakers on her feet.

"If you want to go for a walk, ask me. I will take you out."

Her jaw thrusts forward. "What if I want to walk alone?"

"*Nyet*." I shake my head. "Not allowed. If you leave this house, it's with me. Your choice."

She crosses her arms and purses her lips, clearly torn between wanting to go out and not wanting to yield to my rule. "I'm not begging."

I hide a smile. "I didn't say you had to beg. Just ask. Come, you want to go now? I'll take you out." I walk past my soldiers, who step aside for me, and extend my hand.

She eyes it. "I'm not holding your hand, either."

A laugh bursts out of me, startling my men. Startling me.

She crosses the threshold unharmed this time, a reluctant smile playing on her lips. We fall into step beside each other, and I lead her toward the path into the trees.

"I like you, Alessia," I admit.

"I know," she says, which makes me chuckle again. "Not enough to let me go, though?"

I don't answer because the truth is the opposite. I like her too much to let her go. But telling her that won't help my case any.

And I will let her go. I know that. I think she probably knows that, too. Otherwise, I think she'd be freaking out quite a bit more than she is.

I take her on a hike to the lake, because I figure if she was dying for fresh air, a short walk wasn't going to cut it.

It's a forty minute walk, and I'm surprised to find her short of breath and stopping to rest fairly often.

"Is this the diabetes?" I didn't know it caused shortness of breath and fatigue. "Do you need a snack?" I curse inwardly for not having food on me. "Let's turn back."

"No, I'm all right," she pants, hands on hips like she's exhausted. "It's beautiful out here. I'm having a good time."

"Does exercise affect your blood sugar?"

"I'm fine. Really. Let's keep going."

I'm torn between wanting to please her and worrying over her health. I concede, walking slower and taking breaks. When we arrive at the lake, the delight on her face makes me decide it was worth it.

"Vladimir! This is beautiful! I didn't know you had a *lake*. Wow."

"You like water?"

"Who doesn't? This is incredible. I can't believe you didn't build your house closer."

I want to reach for her pretty face, stroke it, but there's distance between us now that she's no longer tied up. No longer eating from my hand.

I'm wooing her now, not forcing.

"I built where architects advised, for flooding reasons. But yes, it's beautiful. It's why I chose this land to buy."

"Do you swim here?"

"Sometimes. It's cold."

She chuckles. "I'll bet." She finds a rock near the shore and sits on it, facing the water. "I could sit here all day."

I sit beside her.

It's funny. I had this big house built here near the lake,

125

but I've never spent any time here enjoying it. Not until now.

I breathe in the fragrant summer air, listen to the sound of birds and insects calling to one another.

I want to pull Alessia onto my lap and inhale her scent, too, but I keep my hands to myself.

"What did you say to the guard who stopped me?" She breaks the peaceful silence.

"I told him never to touch you again."

Her full lips curve up.

"And when I stabbed you—what did you say to Mika?"

"I gave him earful."

"I recall. What about? Letting me get a knife or for holding a gun?"

"What do you think?" I ask.

She turns and blinks at me. Her brown eyes are golden in the sunlight. She wears no makeup, and looks as fresh and beautiful as a model.

"You already know the answer."

"Holding the gun?"

"Pointing it at you." The memory rushes back. I'd felt no pain from the stabbing in the moment. All I experienced was the stark fear of Mika firing that gun, either on purpose or by accident. No kid should hold a gun—I don't even know where he got that one. "Christ," I mutter, shoving my fingers through my hair. "He could've killed you."

Alessia leans against me, her shoulder pressing against mine. "I like you, too, Vlad."

Shock registers before the pleasure that blooms in my chest.

"When you're not being a dick."

One of those unexpected laughs bursts out of me.

Christ, I don't know when I've laughed last. I never laugh. Like Mika, I grew up too fast. I don't remember when or if play and laughter were part of my experience.

Yet here I am under the wide blue sky with the most beautiful, easy to be with girl on the planet.

Laughing.

It doesn't feel real.

CHAPTER 11

 *lessia*

"ALESSIA."

I don't think Mika's used my name before. I'm glad he's warming up. We had our morning study session and then he disappeared for a while. Now he's shown back up in the living room. He crooks a finger at me. "Want to see something?"

Does the Pope wear a pointy hat? I'm bored out of my skull locked up here. Vlad's been working all day in his office. I scramble off the comfortable easy chair I'd settled into. "Yes. *Da.*" I've started on my Rosetta Stone Russian lessons. I wish I could just download the language into my head like they do skills in *The Matrix*.

I follow Mika to the back wing of the mansion. To what appears to be more of the "servant's quarters." Zoya's domain.

Mika takes me into the laundry room and points. There, bounding in and out of a wicker laundry basket full of towels, is a litter of black and white kittens. Their tiny mews make me laugh.

"Awwww," I exclaim, crouching down to pet a tiny head with my index finger. "They're so sweet." I pick one up and hold it to my chest. It starts purring immediately. "Is the mama cat Vlad's?"

"I don't know."

Zoya comes in, her expression severe as always. She says a few harsh words to Mika.

"She says she has to get rid of them before Vlad finds out. I think the mama is hers."

I grab the laundry basket protectively. "No way she's getting rid of them." I pick it up. "Ask her if I can keep them."

Mika's eyebrows shoot up. "All of them?"

I don't really want to keep *all* of them, but annoying Vlad is my only diversion these days. I think having five rambunctious little kittens tearing around his bedroom is a perfect way to drive him crazy. "*Da*," I say.

I am perfectly willing to go up against him on this issue, even if Zoya isn't.

Mika says something to Zoya who looks at me doubtfully.

I kick up my chin. "The kittens are coming to my room," I announce. "Vlad can deal." Maybe I can use this as a bargaining chip to get my own bedroom. Lord knows sharing a bed with Vlad is a dangerous proposition. If we have a repeat of the other night's performance featuring his tongue between my legs, I won't be able to resist him.

"Will you ask Zoya to bring a litter box to my bedroom?" I ask Mika as I breeze out the door carrying the kittens.

I leave Mika and Zoya discussing the situation in the laundry room.

In the bedroom, I close the door, turn on the television and let the kittens explore. They are the cutest things I've ever seen and they totally brighten my day. Even if I hadn't wanted to annoy Vlad, having them in the room is a delight.

Zoya installs the litter box in the en suite bathroom. I can't understand what she's saying, but there is much hand-wringing and clucking about it. She's definitely worried about Vlad's reaction.

"Don't worry," I tell her in English. "I'll handle Vlad."

She catches his name and bobs her head, talking some more. Finally, she leaves.

I sit on the bed and watch TV, holding various kittens on my lap. When Vlad comes in, there's one on my shoulder, one on my chest and two in my lap. The fifth one is curled up on Vlad's pillow.

He stops short. "What...?"

I smile broadly. "You have kittens! I'm keeping them all."

The kitten on my shoulder is batting at my hair. I laugh and pet her.

I expected Vlad to be annoyed. Instead, his expression softens and he just gazes at me for a moment. "That's cute," he says, surprising me.

"Aren't they?"

He shakes his head, his lips curving into a slight smile. "Not them. You. You with them. Very cute."

I'm taken aback. "So I can keep them?"

"*Da, printsessa.* Whatever makes you happy."

"Can I get a puppy, too?" I press.

He just grins. "Now you're just testing me. Do you even want a puppy?"

"Maybe not until the kitties have grown up a bit," I concede.

Vlad's smile grows even warmer. The lines on his face, softer. He's a different man like this—younger and more handsome. Almost boyish.

I pick up the kitten on my chest and hold it out to him. "Hold one. They're so sweet."

"Okay." He's so agreeable. He takes the kitten and puts him on his chest, rubbing under its chin to make it purr.

It's ridiculous but I fall a little in love.

I don't want to.

He certainly doesn't deserve it.

But I can't help it.

He's so damn likeable. And the fact that he's also an asshole holding me against my will, the fact that he's a criminal, capable of great violence should be a turn-off. But it's not. Maybe because I come from a long line of men like him. And if we do fall for men who are just like our fathers, then he fits the bill.

He may not be Italian, but the rest is all there.

Dangerous. Powerful. Cunning. Unyielding.

Yet gloriously protective and equally kind.

I peer at him. "You're cute with a kitten, too," I tell him. "But don't think this means I'll have sex with you."

He just smirks. "You will, *zaika*. You'll beg me for it. And you will like it."

Vlad

AFTER THE INITIAL deposit of a quarter million, I get a wire for the rest of the six million from Alessia's brothers. All of it.

It's a smart move on their part. Give me the lump sum at once and use it as leverage to get me to send her back.

It won't work, of course.

I refuse to let it make me feel guilty.

 *lessia*

CURLED up on the comfortable black leather sofa in Vlad's opulent living room, I practice my Russian with the Rosetta Stone.

Mika snickers at my accent.

I repeat it, watching for his approval until he nods.

It's been three days since we arrived and we've settled into a routine with his tutoring. I teach him for a few hours and then he helps me with my Russian. I have the Rosetta Stone and also a translating app. Vlad somehow figured out how to give me a tablet that accesses only certain websites, but I can't get online to do anything else. I can't figure out how he did it, but I think he must be pretty tech savvy. The way his fingers fly over the keys on his laptop, he definitely seems at home.

He works long hours in his office, bent over the laptop or pacing around on his cell phone.

In the afternoons, he takes me out to the lake—my favorite time of the day. Yesterday, I found a garden bench had been placed in a shady spot halfway to the lake.

"Is this for me?" I gasped when we came upon it.

Vlad kept the stoic Russian mask on. "Rest," he ordered, rather than just admit to the kind deed.

I sat, because I did need a rest, then scooted over and patted the place beside me. When he sat down, I pecked him on the cheek. "Thank you."

He didn't answer.

"It's okay to admit there's actually a nice guy under that asshole front you wear," I told him.

"No," he grumbled. "There's definitely no nice guy. I just don't want you to die of exhaustion."

So he said, but when we arrived at the water's edge, I found another surprise. One of those rustic porch swings had been placed right by the rock I usually chose to sit on.

Because I don't want to be touched by Vlad's efforts, I've upped my demands and complaints. I need new music. New clothes—when will he take me shopping? I need a Kindle and romance novels. I want to send letters home.

He doesn't concede to anything, nor does he get annoyed. He just gives me his game face and tosses out orders to keep me in line.

I screw around on the tablet, trying to hack into the internet. Seriously, if he figured out a way to limit it, I can figure out the way to get past it.

"What's the WiFi password?" I ask Mika casually. You

never know. I might trick him by acting like it's a normal request.

No luck.

The boy grimaces and his ears turn red. I feel bad for even asking.

"I'm just kidding. Can I borrow your tablet?" I hold my hand out like I expect him to pass it over to me.

He hugs it to his chest. "Mine doesn't have access, either," he says.

I can't tell if it's true or not. It would make sense, though. Vlad shouldn't trust Mika not to help me, especially when I'm winning the boy over more and more every day. "Only to games and TV."

I sigh and Mika flushes some more. I'm a bitch because I pretty much just asked him to betray the father figure I've been hoping he'll bond to. It's so wrong of me.

"It's okay," I tell him. "I don't want you to feel caught between the two of us. It's not fair to you."

Mika looks at me, his blue-green gaze earnest. "Vlad says he will let you go," he says.

I nod. "I know. I believe him. Do you?"

Mika swallows, but nods. Then he shrugs. "I don't know him so very well, though. Only a few months now."

"I'm sure he's dangerous," I say. "But not to us." I point between the two of us.

Mika studies me intently, as if measuring the truth of my words. Then he nods.

Outside, I hear the gravel crunch as a large truck pulls up. I go to the window to look out. The driver pulls in, then backs up to turn. He must be an idiot, because he backs up way too quickly and totally smashes into one of the cars in the circular drive.

The men on the porch yell. Security guys pour out from all sides, swarming around the vehicle. I watch for a moment, fascinated, thinking this would make an excellent Trojan horse style invasion.

And then it occurs to me.

I don't need armed men to pour out of the truck. All I need is this distraction. No one is guarding the front door right now.

Mika's standing up to look out the window, as well. "Go get Vlad," I order him.

The moment he's out of sight, I shove my feet in my sneakers and dart for the door.

It's some kind of miracle—no one notices. They're all gathered around the accident, yammering. Vlad's already out there, too. He must've exited from a different door. I duck behind the hedges and move swiftly, keeping close to the mansion until I hit the edge, then I dart for the trees.

Vlad's place is out in the country. I will have to hike quite a ways, which sucks with my kidney condition because I get short of breath. But maybe once I hit the main road, I can flag down a car. Not speaking Russian is another serious hitch in my plan, but I've memorized the word for help in Russian—*pomogite*—and I'll just keep saying it until they figure out how to help me.

A half an hour later, I'm sweaty and tired but on the main road. I don't dare stop moving. Panting from the exertion, I wave my hand at every car that goes by, trying to flag one down as I jog along the road.

I'm hoping I'll look desperate and out of place and that

will make someone stop to find out what in the hell is wrong with me.

And then I'm totally in luck because a Russian police car pulls up and two men get out.

"Thank God," I say. "Pomogite. Pomogite."

They jabber at me in Russian, dour sounds coming from harsh, angry faces.

I point down the road toward Vlad's place. "*Zaklyuchennyy*." It's the word for *prisoner*. At least I hope I'm saying it right. It's another one I memorized in case of escape.

They repeat it back. "*Zaklyuchennyy*?"

"*Da!*" I bob my head and point frantically toward Vlad's mansion. "*Zaklyuchennyy*." We need to get the hell off this highway before Vlad figures out I'm gone and comes looking for me.

They speak rapidly to each other in Russian, and then one of them gets on the radio on his phone.

"Yes, let's go." I go to their car and throw open the back door, climbing in the back seat.

"*Nyet*, blah blah blah," one of them scolds me in Russian.

"*Da*," I insist.

They speak together again in Russian, then the officer next to me leans his face down and nods his head, saying something. He slams the door shut and leans against it.

Come, the fuck on.

Get in the car and drive me to the station. We need to call my brothers. Get me on a plane off this continent. Quickly.

I knock on the window.

The cop ignores me, his backside pressed against the freaking window. I can't even open the door now to get his attention. I tap again.

No answer.

Shit. Cops are probably owned by the *bratva* in Russia. Which means I'm screwed.

I try to open the door, but the cop's body blocks me. I slide over to the other side and, surprise, surprise, the other cop has that one blocked, too.

Another vehicle approaches, then screams to a stop, wheels squealing.

Fuck. That has to be Vlad.

I hear Vlad's angry voice and then the cop moves.

Oh hell.

The door flies open.

I stare up at a very angry Russian.

"Come." He beckons to me.

I appreciate that he doesn't manhandle me much anymore, but I'm not going to make this easy on him.

Just in case he doesn't own the cops and I misread the situation, I shriek, "*Zaklyuchennyy!*" again, as loud as I can.

Vlad gives me a withering look. "Who do you think called me, *zaika*?"

Right. I figured.

"Now get out. If I have to lift you out, your punishment will be far worse."

My stomach flutters at the word *punishment.*

I'm half dizzy from the adrenaline. My hands shake as I reach for the door handle to boost myself out.

I'm scared, for sure. I'm not sure what Vlad will do to me.

I'm not terrified, though. He's not cruel. I'm sure of that.

The moment I'm on my feet, Vlad throws me up over his shoulder and carries me to the car. I claw at his back with my nails, not because I think it will do any good, but because I'm not going to go like a limp fucking doll. Especially not in front of the good-for-nothing corrupt police assholes who sent me back to him.

When he sets me down, I slap his face.

Or at least I try to. He moves lightning fast and catches my wrist. "No. Don't make it worse for yourself. You are already in so much trouble."

Vlad

I PUSH Alessia into the passenger seat of the car. "Don't run. Don't fucking open this door. Do not test my temper."

Looks like she's back to being my prisoner.

I won't pretend I won't love stripping her bare and tying her up. I won't pretend I won't love having her at my mercy.

But this is a huge fucking setback as far as our relationship goes.

And I can't believe I'm even thinking that word. We don't have a fucking relationship. She's my prisoner. She may be my wife, but it wasn't by choice. I know that. I need to stop pretending any different.

"You had your insulin with you?" I demand. I already know the answer. She has jack shit on her, and that's what really upsets me.

What if the police hadn't been driving by? What if she'd been out here for hours? I've already seen how breathless she gets when hiking. She has no food on her, no insulin. She could have fucking *died.*

"No," she admits with a grumble. Her arms are crossed over her chest and she's acting sullen, but I saw her hands shake when she got out of the police car. She's afraid of me.

I tear back to my place. "Don't move," I growl when the car stops. I get out and stalk around. Open her door and pull her out. Hoist her over my shoulder again.

Control issues.

Yeah, I have them.

Sue me.

Being in control of Alessia intoxicates me. I tried to do things the right way. Give her space. Let her adapt.

Now she needs a strong hand.

I seem to recall she enjoys it, so I don't have to feel bad.

I carry her into my room and drop her on her feet. The kittens tumble out of their basket mewling, but we both ignore them. Holding her gaze, I unbuckle my belt and pull it from the loops.

Her eyes widen and she stumbles back, breath short.

"Clothes off." My command is short and harsh.

She must be genuinely afraid, because I watch the defiance drain away. She yanks her t-shirt over her head and throws it on the floor. Kicks off the sneakers next. Then the jeans come down.

"All of it," I order when she stops.

Lips tight, she unsnaps her bra and lets it fall to the floor. I don't wait for the panties. I decide I want to strip her of those myself. I reach for her and she flinches, but I catch her wrist and drag her body up to mine.

"Hands together," I murmur, like this is love not war.

Perhaps it is.

Her bare breasts graze my ribs. She's panting, eyes dilated wide.

Not narrowed. Fear causes the pupils to narrow. Excitement causes them to dilate.

My cock, already swollen in my jeans, gets chubbier. I pull her wrists up, my touch gentle now. Without looking away from her lovely, startled doe eyes, I toss one end of my belt over the rafter on the ceiling and pull the end of the strap through the buckle so it's caught tight.

I lift her unbound wrists to the end of the belt. "You hold this strap. You let go, I take the strap down and use it on your ass. Understand?"

"Vlad." There's a pleading quality to her voice that I rather love.

I put a knuckle under her chin. "Do you understand?"

"Fine. Yes. I understand." She reaches up to grip the end of the belt. It lifts and separates her breasts in the most alluring way.

I hook my thumbs in her panties and take my time slowly pulling them down as I drop to a crouch in front of her. She steps out of them and I slap her legs open. "Spread them, *printsessa*."

She widens them a foot apart. I slap higher, catching her inner thigh. "Wider."

Her belly shudders as she opens them further.

I rub two fingers between her legs, gratified to find her wet. "You're excited about your punishment."

She makes a dissenting noise, but doesn't actually speak.

I slap lightly over her clit and she mewls softly, skittering her legs back together.

"Open them." I put enough sharp dissatisfaction in my tone that she responds instinctively, immediately opening her legs.

I come to stand, dragging my fingertips up her inner thigh as I do, then palming her ass in a rough squeeze. I stroll around behind her and grip her hips. "Push that ass out. Arch your back. If you hold your position like a good girl, I will only use my hand."

This time the mewl is unmistakable.

And adorable.

I smack one side of her ass, hard.

She shivers.

I smack the other side.

"There is no running away, Alessia," I tell her, holding her hip with one hand and applying my hand with more purpose.

She gasps and flinches under the spanks, but holds still. I redden the lower half of her ass, enjoying the spring of her cheeks under my palm. The sound of my slaps in the quiet room. The satisfying sting on my own skin.

"You are my wife. You will stay with me until I grow tired of you."

She makes that dissenting sound in her throat again.

I stop spanking and reach around to cup her mons, using my grip to pull her ass back against my lap. With the other hand I cage her throat. "I took you as tribute for the lives taken from me," I remind her. "I did not take your brother's life. I will not take your life. You'll give me this time as my due."

She goes still, although her pulse is frantic beneath my thumb. Her pussy's soaking wet, too. She works to swallow. I stroke along her sopping slit. I move my hand from her throat down to her breast, which I squeeze roughly.

"So be a good girl. Take your spanking." I slap her pussy. Fist my hand in her hair and tug her head back over my shoulder. Another pussy spank.

She moans.

"I know you like to have your pussy spanked." Another slap.

I step back and start another round on her ass, slapping the pink into her cheeks until she's dancing on her toes.

Then I reward her with more stroking. "You're doing a very good job staying in place, *printsessa,*" I murmur, my lips at her ear. "A very good job." My middle and index finger glide up and down her swollen flesh, stopping to circle her clit. "When you're ready for me to give you satisfaction, just ask."

She turns her face away. There's a blush on her cheeks, down her neck.

"I won't make you beg. I won't even make you apologize. I will put my mouth between your legs and lick you until you scream. And then I'll show you what I can do with my cock. All you have to do is say *da*." The whole time I make that promise, I circle her clit with the pad of my middle finger.

When she doesn't answer immediately, I remove my touch.

"*Da,*" she answers quickly.

I'm not a religious man, but I'm willing to praise Jesus, Mohammad and every other known figurehead. I need to be inside this woman with a clawing desperation.

I reach up and wrap a hand around her wrists. "You can let go," I murmur in her ear.

Her hands slide down the belt as she releases her tight grip. I catch her up in my arms and drop her onto the bed.

"Spread your legs," I say thickly. I can't wait to feast between them. I slide my hands under her heated ass cheeks and squeeze as I lick into her.

She's on fire—so sensitive she nearly pops off the bed every time my tongue makes contact. I have to hold her pelvis down, pin her in place to give her the pleasure she deserves. I swirl my tongue up and around her clit, flick it with the tip. Penetrate her with a finger.

I have her orgasming in less than sixty seconds. I go in for a second round.

Only then do I trust myself to unbutton my jeans and free my erection. Her gaze stays on my cock, and she watches, cheeks flushed as I slide my fist along my throbbing length.

I climb onto my knees and tower over her, jacking my dick.

"Do you have a condom?" Her voice almost sounds shy.

Right. Condom. She can't get pregnant for some reason.

"*Da.*" I back off the bed, stripping my shirt over my head as I walk. I get a condom from the dresser, then shuck my jeans and boxer briefs.

And then I can't hold back anymore. It's been too many nights of torture. My cock aches so badly. I need to be in her with a vengeance I can't deny. I'm more animal than man when I get back on the bed. I grasp her hips and flip her to her belly, then pull her hips up until she comes to her knees. When she tries to come onto her hands, too. I force her chest back down.

"I want this ass up," I tell her, bringing my thumb between her crack.

She lets out a protesting squeal, but it sounds more wanton than anything.

I slap her ass. "If you ever leave the house without insulin and a snack again, I will fuck this ass raw."

It's a vulgar threat but my brain stopped functioning the minute she said yes. The only thoughts running through my head now are *Fuck her now. Fuck her hard. Fuck...her.*

Yeah, I'm dying for her.

I rub the head of my cock over her entrance and push.

Blyat, she's tight. I barely get the head in even though she's wetter than an ocean.

I push harder and she mewls, panting.

I haven't felt a girl this tight since—

Oh shit.

I grab her long, shiny hair and pull it back over her shoulder to see her face. "Alessia." My voice is pure gravel. "You're not a virgin?" I can't stop the alarm from ringing out through my thick accent.

"No," she breathes and I relax. But then she says, "I've had sex before."

I stop again. "How many times?"

"Two."

I want to laugh.

And cry.

I stroke my hand up the hollowed arch of her back, reach around and toy with her nipples. Inch in a little more. Sweat gathers at my hairline from the pressure of holding back.

"Okay, baby?" I ask.

"Yes. It's good, Vlad. Keep going."

I grip her hips and thrust in deep all at once.

She doesn't scream. Her moan sounds happy.

Thank fuck.

Fingers digging into her flesh, I let my passion loose, pumping into her. I'm already dizzy, my balls so tight, cock so hard. I bump her ass with my loins hard. Harder. I like the slapping sound it makes, like another spanking.

She must like it, too, because she moans and gasps into the bedcover, fingers clawing at the fabric.

I hold her nape, bunch my hand into her hair. I massage the back of her scalp the way she likes it, all the while fucking her so hard the bed rocks.

"Oh God," she moans. "It's so good."

Satisfied I'm not hurting her, I let loose even more, pulling her ass back to meet each of my brutal thrusts. Her cunt is tighter than a glove around my rigid cock, and I've never felt such glorious satisfaction before.

"Alessia," I find myself panting. It's like an invocation. I'm having more than a spiritual experience. My world is fucking cracking open. "*Alessia.*"

"Vlad, please. Yes. Oh God."

I'm way too rough, but I can't help myself. I pound into her until she screams my name. Until I forget who I am.

What I am.

Until lights explode behind my eyes and I come like a fucking freight train.

CHAPTER 13

 lessia

I TOTALLY BEGGED.

I'm not even embarrassed because it was so good it was worth it. I actually had no idea sex could be so incredible. I'm going to become an addict. I won't be able to leave Russia because my body will want to stay enslaved to Vlad.

I'm so screwed. Ha. Literally.

Especially when he suddenly becomes infinitely gentle.

His cock still throbs between my legs. We both came. We both saw. I think Vlad conquered, but I was happy to become his conquest. But now he eases me to my belly, following me and covering my body with his own. He strokes my hair back from my face and lays kisses along my jaw, my shoulder. My back. All the while, he keeps rocking that big Russian cock of his between my legs. Lazy-like. He's the ocean and I'm the boat. And he's definitely a ride I don't want to get off.

I moan softly.

"Are you okay, Alessia? Did I hurt you?" he murmurs, lips still trailing across my skin. "I'm sorry I was so rough."

Cristo, this man is going to slay me right here. The tenderness after the heights he just brought me to is too much.

"Mmm," is all I can give for an answer.

"Roll over." He pulls out and tugs on my shoulder and rolls me to my back. "I want to look at you."

He studies my face. I don't mind looking at him, either. The crude tattoos. The muscles. The stark masculinity. That ice blue gaze. Especially the way he's looking at me now. Like I'm the most beautiful woman on the planet.

His cock nudges my entrance again, and I sigh when he spears me. He's only half-hard now, but it still feels so good. As he rocks, he lowers his face slowly to mine. Hesitates, hovering just above me.

And then his mouth descends. He claims my lips and shoves in sharply.

I moan against his lips. Move mine in concert with his. It's bizarre that our first kiss comes last. After everything else—spanking. Oral. Fucking. Everything but anal, really.

Well, everything I know about, which probably isn't that much, as he just showed me.

The kiss goes on. His lips devour. Teeth scrape over my flesh, tongue dips in and twines with mine.

His cock hardens again inside me.

And then, abruptly, he ends it. Comes up for air and stares down at me. Strokes my cheek with his thumb.

I lean into his touch.

"Don't move," he murmurs after a long moment.

He regretfully pulls out and walks to the bathroom. He returns without the condom, carrying a wet washcloth and my med kit. He climbs up over me and cleans between my legs as he drops kisses over my breasts, across my throat. Between my breasts.

Then he checks my blood sugar and kisses the place he pricked.

Hungry, I roll off the bed and reach for his t-shirt to pull over my head.

"Uh uh," he barks from the bed. "No clothing for you. You lost privileges."

I can't take him too seriously. I may have been afraid when he brought me in, but after the tenderness he showed me, I know where I stand.

"Oh yeah?" I purr. I go back to the bed and straddle his waist.

He grips my ass and hikes my hips up to grind over his cock. When I rub my bare breasts against his face, he groans. "You have me right where you want me, don't you?"

"Do I?" I ask innocently.

He catches my jaw and brings my face down for another hard kiss. "I'd probably give you anything you asked for right now."

"Set me free."

He leans his forehead against mine. "Not that."

"Let me call my brothers."

He groans and rolls his eyes, but appears to be thinking.

He's totally going to let me.

"*Nyet.*"

What? Seriously? "Why not?" I demand.

"Because it will make you sad. I want to make you happy right now."

Damn. It's hard to argue with that logic, since I cried last time I saw them on the screen.

This guy is pretty sweet for a kidnapper.

"I do have one small surprise for you," he offers, palming my breasts and teasing the nipple with his thumb.

I brighten. "You do?"

"*Da.*"

I wait, but he continues toying with my nipple. Finally he sighs and lifts me off his lap and onto my feet. "I don't want to leave you." He climbs off the bed to stand.

"So take me with you," I offer brightly.

He closes his eyes and shakes his head like it pains him. "You're on restriction, *zaika*." He cradles the back of my neck and pulls me into him, dropping a kiss on the top of my head. "I'll be right back. I promise." He releases me and pulls his clothing on, then leaves me in the room.

I don't hear the key turn in the lock.

I go and check it.

He left it open. Does he trust me to obey him now?

Or he just wasn't willing to lock the door after what we just shared?

Either way, it feels good to me. I'm not going to test it by leaving.

I climb on the bed and lie on my back, staring up at the

ceiling. Vlad's belt still swings from the rafter, which makes me smile. My body buzzes from the orgasms, limbs relaxed and rubbery, skin sensitive.

This is my life now. Vlad's wife, until he grows tired of me.

Is it weird that I don't think it's so bad? That part of me is happy to have the choice removed, to be stuck with this dangerous, beautiful man five thousand miles from home.

Vlad returns shortly, carrying a bowl of yogurt with fruit in it and my tablet, which I had left in the living room.

"That's your surprise?"

"No. It's coming. This is to tide you over until dinner. I know you're hungry."

I take the bowl gratefully. I am hungry, actually. Starving. "How do you know?" I peer up at him as I take a spoonful.

He shrugs. "I know you."

I know you.

Simple words. A simple sentiment. Yet it strikes me at that moment how true his words are. He does know me. Not even my own mother knows my rhythms and needs as well as this man.

I shovel another bite into my mouth. "So dinner's coming?"

"*Da.*"

"And the surprise."

"*Da.*"

"Is dinner the surprise?" I guess.

His lips twitch. "Maybe." He opens my tablet and swipes across the screen. As usual, his fingers work quickly. A few moments later, music fills the room. It's Daft Punk—one of the songs I requested. I'd made the longest list I could come up with, with many obscure songs and bands, just to annoy him.

"My playlist?" I guess. "Is this the surprise? When did you have time to download it?"

He watches me, affectionate amusement making the normally harsh planes of his face appear soft and youthful. "I had it on my computer. I just transferred it over."

"Thank you." I take the tablet and sit cross-legged on the bed to scroll through. Vlad found every single song I requested. And loaded them in the exact order I wrote them down.

Satisfaction flows through me. And something else. Something dangerous...happiness.

Thirty minutes after Vlad came back, a knock sounds at the door. "That's our dinner," he says. "Go wait in the bathroom."

"You could just let me wear clothes," I protest, hopping off the bed.

"*Nyet*. No clothes for you." He slaps my ass and I scurry forward, out of his way.

I wait in the bathroom until he calls me back and then I burst into laughter when I see what's on the tray.

French fries.

Home made, not the frozen kind. Fresh out of a fryer.

"Is this my surprise?"

Vlad nods. "You said you like french fries. I ordered a fryer and Zoya made them fresh for you."

I laugh, and then suddenly I'm crying.

"Alessia?" Vlad crosses quickly over to me and takes my shoulders. "What's wrong? What is it?"

"Nothing. It's just… this is really nice. Very thoughtful. And…" I can't seem to stop the flood of unexpected tears. "I don't want to fall in love with you, Vlad."

Alarm flashes over his face. We stare at each other, both apparently terrified by what I said.

"Don't—" he grits, like speaking pains him. "Don't say that, or I'll never let you go."

"I won't say it," I say quickly, turning away.

He catches me, but doesn't turn me back. Just wraps his arms around me from behind.

A few more tears fall. Emptiness descends. Emptiness, but also surrender. I gave him my vulnerability. He gave me his.

There's a peace that comes with it. He's not letting me go. But he's holding me. He's got me in a way no one has before.

There's something to that, right?

I drag in a shaky breath. Turn around in his arms and lean my head against his strong chest. His heartbeat sounds against my ear.

I do love him.

It's illogical and stupid, but I guess you can't tell the heart anything.

"Come on," he says, stepping backward, but still holding me with one arm. "Try Zoya's french fries or she'll be mad at me for all the work."

I let out a watery laugh. "Are you kidding? I'm going to eat every last one of those fries. Well, maybe I'll save some for Mika."

"I guarantee Zoya made him his own." I hear a smile in Vlad's voice, and I tip my head up to see it.

"Zoya's fond of Mika, right?"

"Da."

"I can tell. That's so sweet, considering how she seems like a crotchety old lady the rest of the time."

Vlad chuckles. "She is a crotchety old lady. But she takes good care of us."

Standing over the tray, I grab a fry and dip it in the ketchup, which also appears homemade. It tastes different, but not bad. "Mmm. She does take good care of us."

Vlad slaps my ass lightly. "Get in bed. I'll feed you."

I roll my eyes, even as I obey. "My hands aren't tied, buddy."

He waggles his brows. "I can remedy that situation."

 *lad*

"How long are you keeping me locked up in here?" Alessia straddles me in bed the next morning and my brain scrambles.

I grip her hips and yank her pussy over my thickening cock. She gets wet immediately, grinding down. Her youthful breasts brush my chest.

"Hmm?" she prompts.

Oh what? Right, there was a question.

"Until I believe you've learned your lesson." I palm her ass, squeezing the ripe flesh until my cock's so thick it hurts.

Alessia sits back. "I won't run away again." Her tone is serious, the teasing quality gone. It has the ring of a promise.

I tug her hips over mine again, but she grabs my wrists to stop me.

"I mean it, Vlad. You have my word. I don't know if that means anything in the *bratva,* but in my Family, it does."

I'm not inclined to believe a woman's promise ever, whether she's Italian or Russian, but I don't say that.

"Why would I believe you, *zaika*?"

"I heard what you said yesterday. You could've taken a life for a life. My brother's. But you didn't. You're just taking this time from me. I'm willing to honor that exchange."

Ah, Alessia. Ever giving. Ever sweet.

I reach up and grasp her nape, pull her face down to mine and kiss her hard. "One condition." I roll our bodies so I'm on top now.

"What's that?" Her cheeks glow with color, eyes are bright.

"You're mine in this bed now. No more refusing me. I want you, I take you. Understand?"

"But I don't have to beg?"

I laugh. It's unreal how this woman can make me laugh. "You *will* beg, *zaika*," I tease. "But you don't have to." I climb off to get a condom. "Don't move."

She stays.

I grab her hips and pull her to the center of the bed. "You are a perfect woman, you know that?"

"Am I?" Delight shines on her face. She's so expressive. So lovely.

"*Da*. Beautiful." I kiss the flat plane of her belly.

"Kind." Another kiss. "Funny." I part her legs and flick my tongue over her clit.

She shrieks and tries to close her legs.

"Uh uh. Keep these legs open or I'll spank that pretty ass of yours again."

Her inner thighs tremble, but she keeps them open, arching and releasing her pelvis as I trace the inside of her labia with my tongue. I torture her until her moans grow high-pitched and desperate, and then I shift up and roll on a condom.

"Mine," I growl as I shove into her.

She doesn't deny it. In fact, she wraps those long legs around my back and pulls me in deep.

 lessia

"WHY ARE YOU NERVOUS, ALESSIA?" Vlad's watching me closely. He just showed the doctor out the front door and now he stands in the doorway. He brought the doctor in to examine me and take my blood work.

The doctor seemed nervous to be here, like Vlad is some kind of dignitary or something. I guess *bratva* is well-respected here. Or maybe he guesses I'm a prisoner and is afraid I'm going to appeal to him for help.

Of course he couldn't know how sexually satisfied this prisoner happens to be.

I pick at a fingernail. My hands are clammy and I have a knot in my solar plexus. It's been eight months since the stage 3 kidney failure diagnosis, and I've managed to keep it hidden from the people who love me. It's like, if no one knows, it's not real.

But maybe this doctor won't find it. Depends on what tests he runs on the blood. "What is he checking for?" I try to sound casual.

I must fail because Vlad's eyes narrow. "What do you know he will find?"

Busted.

I draw a circle with my toe on the living room rug. Mika's listening from his post on the sofa.

"Does this have to do with why you think you can't have children?"

I look up sharply, wondering how he figured that one out.

He shrugs. "Doctor said diabetes shouldn't prevent it, it's just riskier."

I'm cold and sweaty all at once.

"Just tell me, Alessia." There's a pleading quality to Vlad's voice I haven't heard before. Only then do I realize he's a little pale. "Is it cancer?"

Mika puts down his tablet to listen, eyes wide.

Cancer is everyone's biggest fear. That word alone produces fear in the least emotional of people.

"Kidney failure," I say quickly, since he's already gone to the worst. Or what he perceives as the worst.

His brow furrows. "Fuck. A result of the diabetes?"

I nod. "I'm at stage three. Stage four is when you have to do dialysis."

"This is why you're short of breath?"

"Yes."

He rubs his forehead. "Is it..it's not—"

"It's not terminal, no. The next step would be dialysis

and finding a donor match for a kidney transplant. But I'm not there yet."

Vlad seizes on that. "Kidney transplant. *Da*. You don't have to wait for dialysis for this. We'll find you one now."

"No." I shake my head vehemently. "I'm not ready for that. My family...I haven't even told them yet."

Vlad considers me for a moment, absorbing this. "Why not?"

"I'm just not...ready."

"You don't want to deal with it. Don't want it to be real."

Relief that he understands sweeps through me. "Yes. Exactly." I've been so freaked out about the whole thing. About dealing with my family's emotions around it. Having to stand strong against their fears. Their overprotectiveness. And then there's facing the whole kidney transplant thing. Getting on a donor list. Searching for a match. What if we don't find one? My whole life could become consumed by broken hopes and bitter dreams.

Vlad comes over to the couch and sits beside me, then pulls me onto his lap. "You're not alone, *zaika*. This can be handled. I'll handle it, okay? We'll find a match and do the surgery and your life will improve. You can have those babies you want so badly. Go on longer walks."

My eyes sting. I wrap my hand over the top of one of his and squeeze. "I'm not ready," I whisper.

He nods. "I'll take care of it. You'll be ready when it's time," he promises.

I want to believe him. Vlad is the sort of man who gets impossible things done. Like kidnapping a mafia princess and taking her to Russia. Making her fall in love with him.

And I'm relieved at his unemotional response—so different from how my Sicilian family would've reacted. Or at least how I projected they would react.

And maybe finding a donor will be easier in Russia than in the U.S. Lord knows, the corruption here goes far and wide. Maybe Vlad can offer big money to a donor here. Or pull strings to get me to the top of a list. There might be advantages to being in this country. To having Vlad in my corner.

I turn and lean into him, tucking my face into his neck. He continues to hold me, stroking my back and massaging my scalp.

I know this isn't a fairy tale. Vlad isn't my prince. He's definitely no knight in shining armor. But if he thinks he can fix me, maybe he can. I let some of the fear that's been gnawing at me since the diagnosis ebb.

I'll let him shield me from the fears I've been running from for a little while longer…

Vlad

THIS IS A TERRIBLE IDEA.

Alessia shoots me a speculative look as we drive in the back of the limo into the city. Mika's on the seat across from us, watching out the windows.

"Are you taking me shopping?" She's been trying to guess where I'm taking her, and I've been cagey about it.

Mostly because I'm thinking it's a huge mistake.

I rub my forehead. "If you like, yes." Maybe I should scrap my plan and just take her shopping. Nothing makes a woman happy like spending money on her.

Although Alessia might be different, since she comes from money.

I can make Mika happy, then.

"Where are we going? Why do you seem tense?"

The limo pulls up in front of a communist-era government building and stops. Alessia peers out the window, then back at me.

"I think this was bad idea," I mutter.

"What is it?"

Mika reads the sign. "An orphanage."

Alessia's brows fly up. "What are we doing?"

I scrub a hand over my face. "We don't have to go in."

"What were you thinking?" she demands, putting a hand on my arm.

"I just thought..." I sigh. "You might like to hold babies. Rock them. They need volunteers. But I don't want to make you sad. I think this was a bad idea."

Alessia throws her door open and climbs out. I leap out to follow. Why does it feel like my heart's up in my throat?

"I definitely want to volunteer," she says brightly, like I'm taking her to an amusement park or something. Which would've been a far better idea. "Let's go." She grabs my hand and tugs me toward the door.

Mika climbs out of the limo and follows. "Why would you want to volunteer?" he demands.

"Come in, let's find out." She throws the door open and looks over her shoulder at Mika.

He's clearly unenthused about this whole plan. I still have my doubts, too, even though her reaction is positive.

She might be horrified by what she finds in there. If I take the kittens as any indication, she'll probably demand I adopt them all. And all I really know is that I don't want to see her cry again.

I checked beforehand and thought the place looked clean and decent enough for what it is, but she's an American. She may find the conditions inside heartbreaking. But I'm hoping it could become a project she cares deeply about. Something to keep her here. Something to give her a purpose.

My phone rings and I stop when I see it's Victor. I hold up a finger to Alessia, who stops and waits. It's a simple interaction. Basic. Human.

And yet I'm momentarily struck by it.

It's like she's a girlfriend or wife. A real wife. Not a kidnapped mafia princess. Not a prisoner.

Her face is open, kind. She's waiting patiently as I flick my thumb across the screen and answer my *pakhan.*

Victor has questions and demands, as always. Hearing his voice grates on my nerves, even though he's the closest thing I have to family now that my mother's dead.

"I need you here in Moscow, Vlad. Permanently."

"I'm always available to you. I answer your calls, we talk daily. What is this about? Do you trust my work?"

"You know I do, that's why I need you."

This is a generational divide. Or maybe just a product of paranoia as the leader of the brotherhood. He likes to see people's faces. Sniff out lies. Maybe I should teach him how to video conference. "I handled everything we talked about yesterday."

"You are too tied up with your hostage-bride to handle my business affairs," he accuses. "Women have always been your downfall, Vlad. Will I have to clean up a mess from this one, too?"

I bristle. "Sabina was a mistake. This one is business." I shoot a glance at Alessia, the lie sending bile up my throat.

Good thing she doesn't speak Russian.

Mika's frowning at me though. Glowering, actually. If he were a full-grown adult, I'd say he wanted to throat-punch me. I shake my head and point at the phone, trying to tell him I'm just telling stories to Victor. What the boss needs to hear to get off my back.

Bratva are forbidden to marry, so I've already violated code. The code that's punishable by death.

"Sabina is under my protection now," Victor says.

Huh. Okay. Well, who the fuck cares? She's a black widow who preys on men to get what she desires.

"She twisted you around her finger now, eh?" I shouldn't say it. Shouldn't be disrespectful. I'm not pissed that he has a new woman after my mother's death. He's had multiple women all along. My mother was one of a great multitude of lovers. And I'm not supposed to even have a mother according to thieves' code of conduct, but because my mother's the one who got me in with Victor to begin with, he let the connection slide so long as I kept it hidden from all others.

"You'll be respectful when you see her," he snaps.

As if she deserves my respect. The woman manipulated me. Seduced me without telling me she belonged to Zima. Then pretended she was pregnant and asked me to kill Zima to free her. When I refused, she confessed to Zima so he'd kill me.

But considering Zima's dead and I was called back from America, my guess is she manipulated Victor into doing her dirty work when I wouldn't.

"As you wish, *Pakhan*," I agree, though. You don't cross Victor. Not over anything.

Lately I value my life more than I used to.

"You will come to Moscow," he says and I hear the steel in his voice. I irritated him. Now I will pay. "You will come and bring the girl so I can see this pet you have now. And the orphan you brought home from Chicago. Then we will discuss your future."

Blyat.

"As you wish."

"Tomorrow," he says firmly.

"We'll be there tomorrow." I end the call and close my eyes.

"What is it?" Alessia asks.

When I don't answer, Mika does. "He has to go somewhere."

"*We* have to," I correct. Damn. I don't want to bring either of them anywhere near Victor. I didn't want responsibility for Mika. Not to begin with. But now that he's been my ward for these few months, the idea of turning him over to anyone else makes me uneasy. And Victor will want to throw him into the lowest ranks of the *bratva*. Teach him to steal, murder and lie. Just like he did to me. I now wish I'd spent more time teaching Mika to hack.

Then I could make Victor believe he's most useful with me.

"Tonight we fly to Moscow."

Alessia perks up. Whether it's because she sees travel as a better opportunity to escape me or because she's sick of being cooped up in my estate, I can't say.

"Let's go," I say tersely, lifting my chin toward the door. I have bigger problems now than whether my bride gets upset by Russian orphans.

I called ahead, so I ask for the director, who bends over backwards to accommodate us. She leads us down a dank corridor to a large room filled with twenty cribs. And one rocking chair.

One empty rocking chair.

Babies are crying and the room smells like urine. Two hassled workers carry babies from a washroom back to their cribs.

The director points at one of the babies newly deposited in the crib. "This one is clean." She picks up the crying infant and hands it—I can't tell if it's a boy or girl —to Alessia. Taking a bottle from the crib, the director hands it over as well.

The look on Mika's face is pure horror.

Alessia, too, looks shocked.

"This was bad idea," I say out loud. "Come, we go now." My accent is thicker because I got tense.

"No, wait!" Alessia is bouncing up and down making shushing sounds. "I want to stay. You guys can go. Come back for me in a couple hours."

Like hell.

I give her the stink eye to show her I don't trust her

alone for a second, but she's gazing into the baby's face speaking in sweet baby-talk tones. The baby quiets and coos back.

"Want some milk?" she asks it, backing into the rocking chair and bringing the bottle to the baby's lips. "Are you hungry, angel?"

It's hard to believe she's considering escape at this moment. She's totally wrapped up in that baby.

I glance at my phone. I have arrangements to make for our flight and lodging tonight in Moscow. "You stay. Make sure she doesn't try to leave," I tell Mika in Russian.

He wrinkles his nose, but nods in agreement. I forget he's already been on the bottom of the *bratva*. He may not have killed yet, but he's certainly known violence.

I squeeze his shoulder.

No way I'm letting Victor take the kid.

And I'll die before I let him separate me from Alessia.

Alessia

I'M TRYING NOT to cry because I know it will distress Vlad.

The orphanage breaks my heart. Of course it does. These babies don't get enough love or attention or time out of their cribs. At least they seem clean and fed and relatively healthy.

The workers eye me nervously, like I'm a government inspector here to give out demerits, but that's understandable. I'm an American, brought in by a dangerous *bratva* member. I'm sure they don't know what to make of the whole thing. I feed the baby in my arms. I don't want to put her down, but there are other crying babies who need attention, so I spread a blanket on the floor and put the baby on it.

One of the workers points at it and then the crib where the baby came from.

"I know," I answer in English, even though they won't understand a word. "But babies need time out of cribs, too." Not that the concrete floor is such a treat.

I pick up another baby, soaked in urine and feces. I guess they don't use diapers here. They just let them soil the clothes and then change them. I follow the workers to the washroom where they are stripping and washing the babies in giant sinks. They aren't cruel. They coo and sing to them in Russian as they work. But there's just too many babies and not enough workers to go around.

It's tragic.

But I'm honored to be here dressing this little baby. Babies are incredible. So innocent. So beautiful. So present.

Babies don't judge. They don't believe in limitations. I lift the baby to my chest for a snuggle. He smells so sweet. His skin is so soft.

And Vlad brought me here because he knows I love children. It's so thoughtful and touching.

It's hard to believe he's a man capable of murder and violence.

"Mika, what are you doing?" Vlad left the room, but the boy is shadowing me.

He looks up at me, wary.

"Take this baby and get him a bottle. Go and sit in the rocking chair and feed him," I instruct him.

Mika looks like he'd rather lick vomit from the floor.

"Come on. Take him. See if you can figure out why I love babies."

I hide my smile at the dubious expression on Mika's face as he takes the infant from me and returns to the crib room.

The baby cries a little, but Mika figures out how to get him feeding pretty quickly. The triumphant smile he beams at me warms my chest.

I help get the babies cleaned and fed and put down for naps and before I know it, I discover Vlad leaning in the doorway, watching.

Mika rushes over to him as soon as he sees him.

"Has it been two hours?"

He nods. "*Da.* Come, *zaika.* You're probably hungry."

There he goes again.

I walk over and give him a peck on the cheek. "*Spasibo,*" I thank him in Russian. "This is the weirdest, sweetest thing anyone's ever done for me."

He grabs the back of my head and kisses me full on the lips.

Mika shuffles past us, obviously embarrassed by the display of affection.

"Don't ask me to adopt them all," Vlad says gruffly.

"Could we do something for them?" I have to ask. "Provide money to hire another worker? Buy them supplies?"

"We?" His expression is unreadable.

I flush. "I mean *you.*"

"I like *we*." He looks serious. Like it only just struck him that he and I might be a *we*. Which makes sense, since this is a sham marriage.

My cheeks are still warm. "Can we, then?"

He inclines his head. "Whatever you want, *printsessa*. It's yours."

It's not true, I have to remind myself. If it were true, he'd let me call my brothers. Set me free.

But I can't stop the rush of good feelings flowing from my heart.

The sense that while life sucks and there's a lot of sadness in the world, I'm not in this alone. There's someone willing to stand beside me.

CHAPTER 16

 *lad*

BEING in Moscow reminds me far too much of my former life there. The life I never wanted to live. All the terror and anger of my youth, of my mother handing me over to Victor and his *bratva*, nearly drown me every time I'm in this city. Everything I hate about myself is here, too. This is where I first killed. Where I witnessed murder and beatings and learned to steal.

Where I decided that if I didn't want to stay at the bottom of the ranks pushing drugs and prostitution, I needed a skill few had. So I learned how to hack. How to launder money. How to make myself infinitely useful to Victor and the other *pakhans* of Russia.

I liked the fantasy of my estate in Volgograd—the one I never lived in until now. Until Alessia and Mika. I liked pretending I might be something else. A husband. Father, even, or at least a decent guardian to Mika.

But now, being back here in Moscow, everything reminds me of the darkness of my past.

Of who I really am.

And I don't want Alessia and Mika anywhere near this shit. I don't want to bring them to Victor's. Don't want to taint them with what I am and have done. Or expose them to the evil that Victor represents.

Victor, the closest man I have to a father.

A man I hate and still love in a twisted way.

I check into a nice hotel suite downtown, not far from Victor's flat.

Mika turns on the television.

Alessia rushes to open the curtains and look down at the city. "I want to see the city," she says. Always with her demands. It's a game now. She doesn't expect me to say yes, she's just poking at me. The squeaky wheel, making herself heard. Reminding me how much she chafes against my authority.

I like to say *no* as much as I like to say *yes* because she's never upset. She pushes but she's not a brat. And I like to say yes because she's always delighted—she doesn't actually expect it.

I simply like to be her authority. She brings out a different side of me. One I didn't know existed. Where I've felt tarnished and cruel most of my life, with her I am benevolent. Yes, her benevolent dictator. It's a role I rather relish.

"Maybe tomorrow," I tell her. I'm too keyed up to want

178

to let her out of the suite. I need her right here, where I can keep her safe.

"Can I go out?" Mika asks in Russian.

That's right. He's from Moscow, too. I narrow my eyes at him. "Where?" I ask in English. Not for his benefit, but for Alessia's.

He shrugs. He's perfected nonchalance. It's hard to know what goes on in that head of his. I consider. He may have family here. Grandparents, aunts, uncles. Maybe friends.

"Who are you going to see?"

Again, the shrug.

"Mika…" I walk over to him. He flinches. The boy's been beaten too many times. "Tell me the truth. Are you running away?"

His surprise is genuine. "*Nyet.*"

"Do you have family here you want to see?" The thieves' code of conduct requires *bratva* to forsake all family. Maybe Aleksi drilled that into him after his mother left. He might be afraid to tell me.

There's a flicker of something on his face that tells me I'm onto the truth.

I shove my hand in my pocket and pull out a wad of rubles. "You know your way around Moscow?" I ask.

Alessia comes over, hands on hips. She doesn't like it.

Mika's eyes drop to the cash as he nods.

"You know where we are now? How to get where you're going?"

Again, he nods gravely.

"Mika, where are you going?" Alessia demands.

Again with the shrug.

"You have your phone? You know how to call me?"

He nods.

"I don't like it," Alessia says. "He's only twelve years old. You're going to let a kid roam around this city alone at night?"

Mika shifts, brows drawing down.

I consider him. The kid lived on his own in a foreign city. He probably roamed these streets from the time he should've been in school.

I hand him the money. "I want you back by ten. Call me if anything goes wrong. Understand?"

Mika bobs his head.

"But where is he going? Shouldn't we bring him there? I don't like this."

"I'm coming back," Mika assures her. Then stuns us both by wrapping his arms around her for a quick, awkward embrace. We stare after him as he scoots out, head down.

"What do you think he's doing?" Alessia demands.

"I would guess he's seeing family or going back to where he used to live. *Bratva* code requires all members to clear ties with family, so I'm guessing that's why he wouldn't tell me."

Alessia taps her lips with one finger. "But you had a relationship with your mother."

"Yes," I agree. "My mother was lover to Victor, my leader. She gave me up to his *bratva* when I was Mika's age. But because she was his favorite mistress, I was allowed to see her sometimes in secret. And I was given special treatment. Victor sent me to America rather than allow one of his men to kill me."

"Why did he want to kill you? What did you do?"

I grimace. "I was tricked by a woman. It's a stupid story." One I definitely don't want to tell Alessia. "Come"—I beckon her over—"let me check your blood sugar."

I give her a shot and order us food from room service. Enough for Mika when he gets back, in case he's hungry.

When a knock comes on the door, I expect it to be room service.

I didn't imagine Sabina would have the nerve to show up at my door.

She stands in the opening in a designer blue dress and stiletto heels, smelling of perfume and deceit.

"Vlad." She tosses her long blonde hair over her shoulder and attempts to come into the hotel room.

I block her entrance.

She looks nervously over her shoulder. "Are you really going to leave me standing in the corridor where anyone might see me? What if Victor found out?"

Dark rage fills me. Is she seriously playing this game with me again? Now she wants Victor to kill me?

Or me to kill Victor?

Not going to happen. I am not going to engage.

"Get out of here before I call him myself," I snarl.

I sense Alessia behind me. She must've heard the tone of my voice. The need to shield her from this shit is so strong, I take Sabina's arm and push her back out of my doorway to slam the door in her face, but she jumps back in the doorway.

"You know why I'm here. Have you read my letters? Why haven't you helped me?"

"Of course I didn't read your letters. And why would I help a woman who purposely put a death sentence on my head? I don't know what you want, but you won't find it here. Now get out."

Sabina catches sight of Alessia and her eyes widen. "Does your American bride know about our child, Vlad?" she says in heavily accented English. I had no idea the bitch spoke English.

I go hot and cold.

"What child?" I snarl in Russian. "The one you invented to convince me to kill Zima?"

The bitch produces real tears. "I didn't invent her. And I had to put her in an orphanage to save her life from him. Why don't you believe me?"

"Get out." She must see the murder on my face, because she stumbles back, into the hallway and I slam the door.

I stare at it for a moment, a buzzing in my ears.

My child in an orphanage? Could that be true?

No.

It's definitely not true. This woman is a liar. A manipulator of the highest degree. She's playing some new game now and it certainly involves Victor.

And the last thing I need right now is to be tangled up with a woman Victor's put his claim on. I'm doing my best to get Alessia out of his crosshairs.

"Who was that?" Alessia demands from behind me. Her voice is cold.

Blyat.

Women.

~

Alessia

WHAT, the ever-loving hell is going on?

Some leggy blonde shows up to our hotel room and Vlad is suddenly a different man. Angry. Enraged, even.

Clearly she's his ex.

Clearly she still means something to him or he wouldn't be so riled up.

He turns slowly and closes his eyes. "That was the woman who nearly got me killed. She's a conniving bitch, that is all."

"Obviously she means something to you or you wouldn't be so upset." I'm not feeling so calm and collected myself. I'm shaky and cold. My hands are clammy. My stomach is in knots.

"*Nyet!*" he explodes, proving my point. "She means nothing. If she were a man I would kill her for her trickery."

He sucks in a deep breath, like he's trying to get a hold of his temper.

"Is it true what she said? You have a child with her?" The woman said that much in English, obviously for me to hear.

I don't know why that hurts me so much, but it does. It cuts right to the core. I guess because I can't have babies. And maybe this afternoon I did conjure some stupid fantasy about Vlad and I adopting a child from that orphanage.

Vlad grinds his jaw. "No. She would say anything. I don't believe her lies."

My stomach twists even more. Something about this feels off. "But you don't know for sure? Don't you think you should find out? Get a paternity test or something?"

Vlad blinks at me. His usual blank expression is returning. "I don't even believe there *is* a child," he says. "Did you see a baby?" he waves his hand impatiently toward the door, but his brows are down, like he's thinking.

Like he hadn't before considered that it might be true.

But then a knock sounds on the door and Vlad answers to room service. He goes silent as we eat.

"Was she your girlfriend?" I can't stop picking the scab.

"Not girlfriend," he clips. "Just sex. Very short time. I didn't know she belonged to a member of the brotherhood. We fucked all weekend. Then I didn't see her for two months. I didn't care. It was sex, nothing more. Then she shows up and says she's pregnant and Zima will kill her and the baby when he finds out it's mine."

I set down my fork, horrified.

Vlad continues, "I said, *how do you know it's mine?* She swore she knew, but I didn't believe her. She was playing me. Asked me to kill Zima. I think maybe he was cruel to her—I don't know. I refused. I gave her money, told her to run away if she's not happy with him, but I wanted nothing to do with her."

I sit staring at him, deeply unsettled. I'm definitely seeing two sides to this story. Yes, it does sound like this woman tried to use him to get away from a bad situation.

And if she asked him to kill Zima, she is everything he says about her. But I also think Vlad had a responsibility if he fathered a child. And maybe he's right. Maybe that was a lie.

He probably knows best.

But my friends back in college had a rule. Pay attention to how a guy talks about his ex, because that's how he's going to talk about you when it's over. And the anger Vlad is showing disturbs me. He's made comments before about women being conniving and manipulative.

I don't want to get lumped into that group the day he decides I'm just like them.

"You don't believe me," he says flatly, then shakes his head and mutters something in Russian, getting up from the little table where we're eating.

"What was that word?" I ask sharply.

"Women," he snaps.

There it is.

Okay. He's pissy. I'm not going to engage anymore. I'll bring it up when he's in a better mood.

I go into the bathroom and shut the door, then start the bathtub. I take my time soaking, giving him space. Taking my own.

Vlad

MIKA COMES IN AT NINE, looking upset.

"What happened?" I ask.

He shakes his head, a little frown burrowed deep between his brows.

"Eat some food," I tell him.

He goes to the table and uncovers the dishes, picking at them, still standing.

I give him a few minutes, then I go over. "Sit." I tug out one of the chairs and drop into the other one.

Mika sits. I can read misery all over him. But getting him to talk is another thing.

"I grew up in the streets of Moscow, too," I offer. "My mother gave me over to the *bratva*, like yours."

He lifts his eyes, wary but listening.

"I still hate her for it."

Alessia looks over from the couch where she was reading one of the romance novels she insisted I download for her.

Mika drops his head, chin wobbling .

I don't touch him. Don't want to stop whatever's going to come out. It will do him better to speak it than to hold it in.

"Your mother is dead," Mika comments. There's a wobble in his voice. He remembers this because we were in the same house in Chicago when she died.

"Yes."

"I wish mine was."

"She did wrong by you," I agree. Wait some more. When he doesn't say anything else, I ask, "Did you go to your old home?"

A single nod.

"Do you have family there?"

He shrugs. Shakes his head. Then offers, "My grandmother."

"Did you go in?"

His face crumples. "No." He's full-on crying now. "I saw her through the window. And I stood there. I stood there for a long time. But I didn't want to go back in. I didn't want to see her."

Now I touch him. I lay my hand on his back. "You don't have to. You don't have to ever see her again, unless you want to. It's your life. Your choice. You have me now. Me and—" I look over at Alessia, but then I stop.

I can't keep her.

I can't promise he has her when it's a lie.

She's going home.

Just as soon as I figure out how to let her go.

"You have me," I say again. "And you have Alessia's money. If something happens to me, it's still yours. I'll show you how to get it. And I won't let Victor take you into the ranks again. He may try, but I won't let it happen. I promise."

Now I've scared the boy by voicing my own fears.

He stares at me with wide frightened eyes, but then he throws his arms around me and presses his head against my chest.

I gulp and rub his back.

Alessia gets up from the couch and comes over. She rubs Mika's head.

He looks up and sniffs, wiping his eyes. "I'm sorry," he says.

"Don't," I say more forcefully than I mean to. "Don't

apologize. Is better to get it out. Leave it behind. Leave it here, in Moscow."

I meet Alessia's sorrowful gaze over the top of Mika's head, and I realize I'm deep in territory I never wanted to enter. The emotional realm. I haven't bared my soul to anyone, much less a twelve-year-old boy, since I was a child. And yet here I am, doing everything I can to make sure Mika gets a better shot at being a decent human being than I had.

And it's because of Alessia. She believed I could— counted on me to do it, so I have.

I may have shown her my worst side when Sabina showed up, but she's also seeing my best. Which admittedly isn't much, but it's more than I've attempted in my entire sordid past.

I reach up and catch her hand and squeeze it and she squeezes back.

For one moment, I pretend we're a strange and unlikely family: Alessia, Mika and me.

But I know it won't last.

It can't.

I already feel the ending screaming up to us without regard to what we accomplish here tonight.

 lad

I'M TRYING NOT to let the tension show, but both Mika and Alessia pick up my mood on the way to Victor's. Mika's pale and subdued. Alessia keeps darting glances my way.

"Why do you have to bring Mika and me?" she asks.

"Victor requested it." I don't look over. I want to hold her hand, but I don't want her to feel how cold mine is. I know something bad is coming, I just can't figure out what it will be.

"Does he speak English?"

"No. You are safe. Say nothing. Look innocent. I won't let him hurt you."

She blanches. "What about Mika?" She heard what I said last night, about not letting Victor take him. I should've kept my goddamn mouth shut. Now they're both worried.

"I will tell him Mika's very valuable. I am training him to hack and he has great aptitude for it. Victor will be pleased. Right now I am irreplaceable. And now that my mother's dead, I think he might prefer to replace me."

Mika watches me intently. When I look at him and raise my brows, he nods.

"You are learning quickly, no? You have great skill already for such a young boy."

He looks doubtful.

"He does not know better. He barely knows how to use a computer. I will teach you these things. I will teach you everything you need to survive the *bratva*. Or if you don't want this, I will help you escape. Your choice. You have choices. And you have me. Don't forget it."

"I want to stay and learn from you." Mika's voice is clear and strong.

I nod. "Good. So it will be. Don't be afraid."

"I'm not," he lies.

We get to Victor's luxury apartment building and are let in by the *bratva* guards at the door. Victor owns the entire building, but he's made the top his penthouse. We take the elevator up and I knock on the door.

One of the brotherhood answers and greets me. "He's waiting for you in his office," he says in Russian. He eyes Alessia with interest, and I put my hand on her nape and draw her closer, showing ownership.

Here she can't be my bride.

Just my property.

"Ah, Vladimir," Victor greets me, standing up. We shake hands. "And who is this?" Victor stands in front of Mika, looking down with a warm, grandfatherly air.

"Mikhael Popov."

Victor cups one side of the boy's face. "Brave boy, living alone in America. You have everything the brotherhood requires."

This is the Victor whose acceptance and attention I craved so badly as a boy. The one I tried so hard to make myself worthy of, to impress.

Mika's not so easily won. "*Spasibo.*"

Victor smiles and straightens, turning to Alessia. "And your Italian prize."

I work hard not to tighten my grip on her nape. He must read my ferocity because he doesn't try to touch her.

A tap sounds on the door and Sabina enters. "I heard you were bringing an American guest. May I borrow her? To practice my English?" To Alessia, she says, "Would you like to join me in the kitchen for a coffee while the men do the man-talk?"

Dammit.

I didn't tell Alessia that Sabina would be here and her poker face sucks. The surprise is unmistakable.

"She is surprised at your English, my dear," Victor says, squeezing Sabina's hand. "Yes, take the girl away. I'm sure she'll be happy for a reprieve from Vlad."

I release her reluctantly.

I don't like this. Not even a little bit. And I can't even figure out a way to send Mika with her to keep an eye on things.

"Don't worry," Victor says. "She can't escape my home. I have men at every exit."

My paranoia is full speed because I'm not sure whether that's intended as a warning to me, or a comfort.

I force my expression into something more agreeable and nod. "Go ahead," I say stiffly to Alessia, who shoots me a furious look before she follows Sabina from the room.

I pull out a chair and sit opposite Victor at his great desk. Time to show him I'm still worth keeping around. And the sooner I do it and get out of here, the better.

Alessia

WHAT. The Actual. Fuck?

Why is Vlad's ex here, leading me to the kitchen?

I'm uneasy as hell. I don't like being separated from Vlad, especially because I know he was uncomfortable about this meeting. I was kept out of mafia business, but I know enough to know that murder and double-crosses happen all the time.

There's a chance Vlad's about to be killed.

Or I am.

And I sure as hell don't trust Sabina or her fake syrupy politeness. She leads me into a lavish kitchen and makes me a cup of instant coffee in the microwave.

Disgusting.

Seriously, Russians need to learn about espresso machines. Today.

I sit at the breakfast bar and pretend to sip it.

She sits beside me, too close. I try to scoot away, and

then I realize she's not elbowing me, she's trying to pass me something.

It's a cell phone.

"Victor said you are prisoner," she murmurs. "This is burner phone. You can call your family for help."

My fingers tremble as I reach for it and tuck it in my purse. Is this some kind of test? What's her angle?

"Why are you giving me this?"

"I know what it's like to be held captive by *bratva*. To be a woman without options." The pretty blonde suddenly looks ancient.

I go still, my suspicions ebbing away. This much, I believe. "Were you captive of Zima?"

She looks over, surprised. "Vlad told you this?"

I nod.

"What else did he say?"

I consider how much to reveal. I want to know the truth about this story. "He thinks you tried to trick him into killing Zima."

"Yes. He's right. Zima was violent man. Cruel. He never let me out. So I looked higher in the organization, sought someone not afraid of him. I tried Vlad. He holds important position in the brotherhood. Is untouchable, they say. The most powerful, second to Victor. And they say he's the wealthiest." She twirls a gold and diamond bracelet around her wrist. "This is important. I wasn't risking my neck to downgrade my condition."

I hide my shock at her admission. Vlad was definitely right about her—she's all about manipulation. Still, I believe her story. I guess because she isn't trying to hide her flaws.

"Zima was away on business, so I seduced Vlad. I tricked him into getting me pregnant. I thought a baby would be enough to persuade him. Men go crazy over reproducing."

She fumbles in her purse and pulls out a photo of a newborn. Her lips tremble when she hands it to me. "But Vlad was heartless. He refused to kill Zima. He wanted nothing to do with me. So I had to look elsewhere." Her gaze travels in the direction of the office.

"Victor," I guess.

She nods. "But Victor would not take me with a child, so I had to give her up. Put her in an orphanage."

My stomach knots.

An orphanage.

God, no.

Vlad's child is in a Russian orphanage? How is that possible? He brought me to one. He's seen how under-staffed they are. How sad the conditions are. Does he really hate this woman so much he would forsake his own child in one?

"Vlad knows this?" I choke out.

She nods, eyes brimming with tears. "I wrote him dozens of letters. Tried to visit yesterday. He won't claim our child."

My own eyes swim with tears. Can this be true?

Sabina grabs my wrist and squeezes. "You are kind. I knew I was right to help you."

The sound of masculine voices comes through the door and she snatches the photo back and shoves it in her purse. "Say nothing," she hisses.

I nod and stand on wobbly legs.

It feels like the whole world is tilting. Sliding and rearranging. I don't know if I even know Vlad. I want this all to be untrue.

I need to get to the bottom of it immediately.

"Come, Alessia," Vlad barks from the doorway.

His authoritative orders don't turn me on right now. They seriously piss me off.

My mouth tightens and I toss my hair, but go to him. As soon as we're in the elevator, he growls, "What in the hell was that about?"

I whirl on him, angry. "You tell me, Vlad. What do you know about Sabina's baby?"

"There's no fucking—" The elevator dings and he shuts his mouth, gripping my upper arm too tight. Mika trails behind us silently. As soon as we're on the sidewalk outside, he says, "There's no fucking baby. The woman is a bag of lies and you are stupid if you believe them."

I'm a firm believer in the no name-calling rules in relationships.

I go ice cold and keep my voice low and dangerous. "Don't call me stupid."

Vlad shoves his fingers through his hair. "I don't mean that. I'm sorry. But I know what is true."

"Do you?" I demand. "She showed me a picture of your baby. The one she *put in an orphanage* because she couldn't seduce Victor with her around."

Vlad stares at me, color draining from his face. "No."

"*Da*," I say, as if throwing his own language back at him makes it stronger. "I saw the picture. She had no reason to lie to me, she was trying to save me from you.

195

Look, she gave me a phone to call my brothers." I wave it in the air like evidence.

Vlad's face goes from pale to fiery.

I take a step back.

"I see. Now I see. Of course you two are plotting together," he snarls. "That's what women do—scheme and trick. Use your beauty and allure to manipulate men and destroy lives. Well, good. You should know, *printsessa*, that calling your brothers was a big mistake. You think your brothers can land in Moscow without *bratva* knowing? Without *bratva* slaying them before their feet touch solid ground? They don't come here without my invitation. You'd better call back and tell them that."

I feel like I've been punched in the gut. Tears burn my eyes. "Fuck you!" I shout. "Seriously, Vlad. Go fuck yourself."

The childish words are the best I can do. The best expression of my hurt and rage.

I turn on my heel and march off down the sidewalk.

I'm certain Vlad will be on me in a moment. That he'll grab me and force me back to the limo. I'm planning on kicking and screaming and biting the whole way, because I've had it with his shit.

But he doesn't.

He doesn't follow.

And I'm relieved at first.

Until I realize maybe there's one thing worse.

Worse than being held prisoner by a man who thinks all women are manipulative bitches.

Being abandoned by him.

Vlad

I WATCH ALESSIA'S BACK, her angry stride, with betrayal shredding through my center.

Another woman playing me for the fool.

Manipulating me. Doing whatever she has to to get what she wants.

Once more I'm the little boy being offered up to the *bratva* to secure my mother's place as Victor's lover.

Let her go, that wounded self screams. Never open your heart to a woman.

But she's Alessia, and I can't stop caring.

"Go with her," I bark at Mika.

He glares up at me, his accusation plain.

I shove a wad of money in his hand. "Keep her safe."

He gives me one last damning look before he obeys, running off after her.

Blyat.

I knew something bad was coming. I thought it would be from Victor. I never dreamed Sabina would continue to cause me this much trouble.

I wave the limo off and walk back to our hotel, my anger fueling my long strides. By the time I get back, I have to know the truth.

I sit down at my computer and hack into public records. If Sabina had a live birth, it will be recorded. And if she gave that child up for adoption, I'll be able to find that, too.

Getting to the bottom of this is the first step to dealing with that woman's treachery.

Alessia

"GO BACK, MIKA."

I walk for at least forty-five minutes—taking rests when I get winded—when I realize that Vlad may not have followed, but Mika did. He's trailing five feet behind me, head ducked like a bad spy.

But he doesn't belong with me, he belongs with Vlad. I have a phone—I can call my brothers. They'll figure out how to get me home safely. But Mika can't come with me. I mean, he could, but I don't think it's the best option for him. And Vlad needs him.

I stop and turn to face him. "Mika, you should go back. Vlad will be worried about you."

He holds out a roll of cash. "He sent me to keep you safe."

I sigh and take the money. If I weren't so pissed, I might find it almost sweet.

Almost.

I sort through the bills. "Is there enough for us to get a hotel room?"

He glances at the rubles and nods.

"Then come on, let's go find a place to stay."

My feet are already tired and we walk around forever because Mika doesn't know where any hotels are, and I don't speak Russian. Eventually, I tell him to hail a cab and tell them to take us to the nicest hotel. I can't tell you how happy I am when they pull up in front of the Moscow Marriott Grand Hotel.

Feels like I'm back in America already.

And what do you know? They even speak English at the front desk.

They don't like my lack of identification and credit card, though. I have to turn on my most convincing rich girl attitude to explain that my wallet was stolen and I lost everything. That I plan to go to the embassy tomorrow, but right now my feet are killing me and I just need a room to put them up.

It works.

In our room, I throw myself on the bed. I'm exhausted and so, so heavy. I'm too numb to even cry.

Mika paces around the room "Should you check your blood sugar?"

"I'll do it in a little bit. Why don't you order us some food?" I suggest.

The phone Sabina gave me burns a hole in my purse, but I don't pull it out. Don't call my brothers. Not yet.

It's not because I'm afraid of what Vlad said, although it is a concern.

It's more the sense that I'm not finished here.

I sort of don't believe it's over between me and Vlad.

And I don't want to leave like this—hating Vlad.

I don't want to leave thinking the worst of him.

Even after the things he said to me.

He's also the same man who handled Mika's tears last night. The man who promised to find me a kidney.

The guy who makes my sexual satisfaction his entire purpose in the bedroom.

Is he perfect?

Hell, no.

Not even close.

But he made me happy.

Happier than I thought possible, especially considering the circumstances. I felt special and beautiful and safe with him.

Cared for. Alive.

Cherished.

And I don't want to get on a plane and never see him again after the way we left things.

But I'm also too angry at the moment to want to work things out.

I have a hot Italian temper and it needs time to cool.

If I'm super honest with myself, I'll admit I wanted him to follow me, to sweep me up and fix it, the way he does. And I wanted to still be mad and resist that fixing until he really proved everything was all right.

But he didn't. He didn't follow, he didn't apologize. He hasn't tried to fix.

At least he sent Mika to keep me safe. I suppose this is a signal. He's really letting me go.

I close my eyes, too tired to even try to think through this shit swamp any more.

~

Vlad

.   .   .

I CALL Mika a dozen times but he doesn't answer. Little prick. I guess he's taken Alessia's side. In the time they've been gone, I hacked the public records.

Sabina has a daughter in an orphanage. And she named me as the father on the birth certificate.

That may or may not be true. The child may be Zima's. It may be Victor's; it may be any other number of men she attempted to manipulate into doing her bidding.

But now I have to find out if it's mine. Alessia would want that.

And that's the thought that sends a lance straight through my heart.

She hates me now after the way I threatened her brother's lives. It's true—Victor would never allow them to set foot in this country alive, but I shouldn't throw such a thing at her. The words were meant to cut.

And clearly they did.

I rub my forehead. Hearing Sabina and Alessia were in cahoots together was a shock to me. It cut deep, especially after the way Sabina ruined my life. But I can't really blame Alessia for accepting Sabina's help. I'm the asshole holding her prisoner. Keeping her from going home.

And if Alessia thought the worst of me, if she took Sabina's side, it's because she has a soft spot for children. I just took her to an orphanage, for fuck's sake. So of course hearing I allowed my own child to languish in an orphanage would be the most horrifying, most damning thing she could possibly hear about me.

That, and me threatening to kill her brothers.

Not my smoothest move.

Fuck.

I really fucked up.

I try to call Mika again. When he doesn't answer, I open up tracking software and find his location.

And then I breathe easy. They are in a nice hotel. Safe.

Good.

Tomorrow morning I will go there and try my best to fix things.

I'll let Alessia go, because she deserves her freedom. But first I must apologize to her. Do my best to sort out the situation with Sabina's child.

I go to bed, but I don't sleep. All night I keep seeing Alessia's horror at my words. The way she stumbled back. The way she flinched as if I might hurt her.

And all night my heart breaks a little more.

I only manage to doze off right before dawn.

And then I'm woken by my phone ringing and Mika's terrified voice. *"I didn't keep her safe, Vlad. Something's wrong and she won't wake up."*

 *lad*

No.

No, no, no.

I talk Mika through giving Alessia a shot of glucagon at the same time I throw on some clothes and run out the door. I stay on the phone with him the whole time, my heart racing faster and faster when he tells me that she hasn't woken up. Hasn't responded.

"I'm going to hang up and call an ambulance," I tell him with a calm I don't feel. "Then I'll call you back."

I hear the wail of a siren as I run into the building. Because I can't stand to wait even an extra few minutes, I carry her down to the hotel lobby in my arms, her head lolling on my shoulder.

Fuck.

Fuck fuck fuck.

Mika's eyes are wet and he's scared. "She said she would check her blood sugar later. And then she fell asleep. I'm sorry, Vlad. I should've woken her up."

"No. It's not your fault. And she's going to be all right," I promise, even though I'm not so sure. Nothing feels right about this.

And it's definitely all my fault.

Alessia

I'M IN A HOSPITAL.

The room comes into focus. The low chatter of Russian coming from the hallway provides the next clue.

Moscow.

I was in a hotel with Mika. And I fell asleep without taking my insulin. But I shouldn't feel this bad.

I feel horrible. Groggy and tired. I try to move and find blood-filled tubes are coming out of my arm. I try to sit up, but I'm too weak. Too tired. I lift my head and look around. "Vlad?"

Movement comes from the corner, and Mika's pinched face comes into view.

"Where's Vlad?"

"He's here, he's talking with the doctors."

"I don't feel right. What's this?"

Mika's chin wobbles. I realize his eyes are red. "You had problem. Your—I don't know how to say it in English —" He touches his back.

"Kidney?"

"*Da*. Kidney failed. Vlad is getting you transplant."

Fear shoots through me like lightning.

A transplant.

Am I already here? It's that bad? This is the place I've been avoiding even thinking about since my diagnosis in Italy. My worst fear.

And now it's happening. My kidney failed. The tubes of blood must be the dialysis. Oh God, my body totally failed me.

And I'm all alone in Russia. No family, no friends.

My vision blurs. I haven't felt this scared or alone this entire time in Russia. Even when Vlad first brought me here and I didn't know what he had in store for me. Nothing compares to the fear I feel now.

I don't like being here in this hospital bed, with tubes coming out my arm, surrounded by nurses who only speak Russian.

"Your brothers are coming," Mika says, as if he guesses my thoughts.

That gives me pause. I try to sit up again, but it's too much work. "They are?"

"*Da*. Vlad called Junior, told him to come."

I sink back, relief pouring through me. I'm going home.

But things with Vlad are too unresolved. I need to see him. I have this sense of being torn in half, ripped right down my center without him by my side.

"Where is Vlad? I need him."

Mika's jaw tenses. "He can't come now. He's with doctors."

I reach out and touch his sleeve. "Is he really here, though, Mika? Or are you lying to me?"

Mika's alarm seems real. "*Nyet.*" He looks over his shoulder. "I will see if the doctors are through with him."

My relief is short-lived, because I suddenly don't want to be left alone in a hospital where I don't speak the language and don't know another soul. "No, wait—" I call as he heads to the door. "Don't leave me here alone. Please."

He comes back. "Vlad is here," he says firmly, like he's afraid I still don't believe him. "He is getting you a kidney."

"Okay. We'll wait for him, then. What should we do?" I look up at the television on the wall.

Mika turns it on and flips through the channels, but all the shows are in Russian. "I know," he says, retrieving his tablet from the chair in the corner. He stands beside me and boots it up. "You like *Friends*?"

I give a watery laugh. I thought I'd seen him watching it back when we were in Las Vegas. He settles the tablet on my lap and we watch together as the time passes interminably slowly.

Vlad

WHEN I WAKE after the operation, my vision swims from the drugs. Even with pain-killers, I feel the incision, the loss of my organ. As my eyes struggle to focus, I hone in on the dark, well-dressed figure looming over me.

He presses the hard muzzle of a pistol against my temple. "Give me one good reason not to shoot you."

Junior. And behind him stand the two Tacone brothers from the Chicago outfit, Gio and Paolo.

I blink up, unafraid. If they want to kill me, they can. I deserve it. I suppose I expected to die by one of their hands the moment I decided to take Alessia.

I wronged their sister and now she lies recovering in a hospital bed because I couldn't even keep her safe.

So no, there isn't a good reason not to shoot me. Not really.

In the corner of the room I catch movement. It's not another brother. It's Mika—pale and scared, eyes as big as his face.

My chest tightens. The kid's been through a lot. First his mother runs out on him. Then the entire Chicago *bratva* is wiped out by the man in front of me. Then I bring him back to Russia and teach him to trust me, only to wind up with a gun at my head and the kid about to witness my demise. Well.

Maybe there is one reason, then.

"She wouldn't want you to," I grate out, my voice rough from intubation.

That much is true. I know her well enough.

"And why is that?" Gio snarls from behind Junior.

My eyes shift to Mika, and I lift my chin in his direction. "She wouldn't want you to orphan him a second time."

Junior shoots a glance at Mika. He's a hard, violent

man. He single-handedly gunned down the entire *bratva* cell. He won't hesitate to kill me if he wants to.

But the moment he sees Mika I know he shares his sister's softness for children. Something changes in his eyes. He considers the boy. "What's your name?"

Mika swallows. "Mikhael."

Junior tips his head in my direction. "You want this guy to live?"

Mikhael nods, a small, rapid movement that doesn't stop.

"All right. Fair enough. I guess I owe you that." Junior pulls the gun away from my head. It disappears into a holster behind his back.

"How is she?" I attempt to move and wince at the pain.

"She'll live." Junior's gaze is hard. "We brought our own doctor and we're taking her home to recover. You go near her again, I'll cut your balls off."

I nod my agreement. I deserve that.

"And stay out of my fucking country. I see you back in the States, you're a dead man. *Capiche*?"

"*Da.*"

"*Da,*" Paolo sneers. "Fuckin' Russian." The Tacones file out of the room.

I close my eyes in relief. Not that they spared me, but at the news that Alessia made it. The transplant was successful and she now has my kidney.

I was able to make up for nearly causing her death.

I'd called Junior and filled him in when I found out her kidney failed. I told him to come right away to take her home after the operation.

Victor agreed to let them come, but only because I

have their money. He doesn't know I returned it weeks ago. I kept Mika's account flush, though.

Before I went under the knife I showed him where it is and how to get to it if anything happened to me. I want him to have options apart from the *bratva* if he chooses.

Alessia

W<small>HEN</small> I <small>WAKE</small> from the transplant operation, I'm alone in my room.

My worst fear again. Where's Mika? Why hasn't Vlad come to see me?

The door opens and three of my brothers march through—Junior, Gio and Paolo.

"There she is, eyes open this time," Gio says with the fake jolliness you use with the ill or underage.

I should be happy to see them, but all I feel is fear on Vlad's behalf. Have they hurt him? I didn't get a chance to tell them not to.

"Where's Vlad?"

Paolo scowls. "In recovery."

I try to sit up, but it hurts too much. "What did you do to him?"

Junior shoots me a strange look. "He just gave you his kidney. Did you know that?"

My mouth falls open. "No." It clicks into place. Why he was with the doctors instead of in my room before the surgery.

"It's the only reason I didn't put a bullet in his head," Junior growls. "That and there's a kid in his room who seems to care about him living."

I blink back my tears. "Don't...don't hurt him. Please."

Junior's expression turns kindly. He squeezes my shoulder. Paolo and Gio move in closer, too. Gio picks up my hand. Paolo pats my leg.

"I'm so fucking sorry this happened to you," Junior says. "All of it." He waves his hand around the room. "It's my fault the *bratva* came for you and I didn't keep you safe. I fucked up."

Tears leak out of my eyes. "Don't." My hands flutter. "Don't blame yourself. I'm just sorry it ruined your wedding."

Junior looks incredulous. "You gotta be kidding me. You're sorry it ruined my wedding? Kiddo..." He touches my cheek with the backs of his fingers. He clears his throat like he's getting choked up. "I'm just glad you're okay. He never hurt you? Because I will seriously tear him limb—"

"*No, Junior,*" I interrupt. "He was actually... pretty sweet. Until we had a falling out at the end."

"We're taking you home, baby sister. We brought our own doctor and we have a private jet," Gio says.

I lay my head back on the pillow and close my eyes. I'm going home.

I should be happy.

But I'm not. I'm just...empty.

CHAPTER 19

 *lad*

"Here, let me take her." I take the baby from Svetlana, the exhausted nanny, and carry her outside. I murmur softly to her and she stops fussing, hiccupping softly into my neck.

Her name is Lara, and she's mine. Seven months old. Prettiest baby I've ever seen.

If it weren't for her and Mika, I wouldn't bother with anything. Eating. Sleeping. Living.

But with children, life goes on. They need us, so we show up.

So it seems.

Every day in Volgograd kills me though. Being at the estate without Alessia feels all wrong.

Everything here reminds me of her and I see her beautiful face everywhere I go.

I walk to the lake and back and the baby falls asleep on my chest. I carry her back in the house and lay her carefully down in her crib.

Mika's at the laptop I bought him with Facebook open.

"What are you doing?" I look over his shoulder and my heart shatters. He has Alessia's profile open. A photo of her in a cap and gown smiles up at me.

Mika slams the lid down like he's been caught watching porn.

"Are you in contact with her?"

He shrugs.

I stand there utterly lost for a moment, not even sure how to reconcile the tsunami of emotions running through me.

Mika steals a glance at me. "Why aren't we going to get her?"

A surprised scoff comes from my mouth. "Not an option. You heard what her brother said. I go to America I'm dead."

Mika looks back evenly. "You're not scared of them."

He's right. I'm not. I peer back at him. "How do you know?"

He gives his characteristic shrug. "You weren't even scared when they had a cocked gun pointed at your head."

"I reconciled myself to death a long time ago. Perversely, I think it's what keeps me alive."

Mika plays with the laptop, opening and closing the lid. "I've seen you scared, though."

"Yeah?" I'm not sure I want to hear where this is going.

"When I pointed a gun at Alessia. And when she was sick."

It feels like my insides are being torn out. "So?"

"So why aren't we going to get her?"

"Because she doesn't want us to. She doesn't want *me* to," I correct, not wanting him to feel abandoned by her, too.

Blyat, he probably totally feels abandoned.

"You never apologized to her," he accuses.

And that's a pain I live with every day.

I shove my fingers through my hair. "She doesn't want to see me. And I'm not going to disturb her peace of mind again."

It's better this way.

The baby wakes up and starts crying again.

I go back in and pick her up. "I know, baby. I know just how you feel."

Alessia

I LIE by the pool on the roof of the Bellissimo and watch the sun set. A waiter brings me a Caesar salad, but I set it on the table beside me untouched. Eating is nothing but a chore these days.

Sondra floats in the water, the only place she wants to be with her big round belly. Nico had a private pool recently installed up here for his wife and sister-in-law.

I'm guessing he and Stefano couldn't stand their women being ogled by the public at the guest pools.

My brothers brought the best nephrologist in the U.S. with them to Russia when they came for me. I was transported on a private jet with the million dollar surgeon looking after me. My recovery has been perfect.

They brought me to Vegas instead of Chicago to recuperate. They figured at the Bellissimo, I'd have a host of employees available to wait on me hand and foot. Or maybe they just wanted to provide ample distraction from my heartache. My mom came too and she's been doing her best to draw me out of my depression. But I can't shake it.

It's been three months and I'm mostly healed from the surgery, and I've been cleared for exercise. My body didn't reject Vlad's kidney. My heart hasn't rejected it either.

The fact that he was a match feels like fate. Like I was destined to be saved by Vlad and his kidney.

It's stupid, but every time I think of a part of him being inside me, keeping me healthy, the noise and anxiety that's been eating at me since I left Russia diminishes.

I haven't heard a single word from Vlad.

No doubt my brothers had something to do with that. But still.

It hurts.

I know I meant something to him. I was more than a monetary transaction or revenge. He gave himself to me. Opened up. Changed.

And I freaking miss him.

I miss the incredible sex. I miss our walks to the lake. I miss the energy—the way I always felt watched, appreciated, admired.

I miss Mika, although he thankfully reached out on Facebook, so we've been chatting. I started tutoring him again, which is the only bright spot to my days. I also made a generous donation to the orphanage in Volgograd, and when they sent the thank you letter, the director wrote: *We were astonished and grateful for your additional gift. Your husband's generosity has already made a huge difference.*

Nico comes out on the deck. He's without the suit jacket but still looks overdressed on the deck of the pool.

Sondra beams at him from the water and he walks over and crouches by the side. When he cups behind her head and pulls her part way out for a kiss, I look away to give them privacy.

I love seeing my brothers in love, but every kiss or touch I witness reminds me of Vlad. And that ache hasn't diminished with time. It's grown bigger.

Nico comes over to the chaise lounge where I'm sprawled, and I keep my head ducked down in the latest Tessa Bailey romance I'm reading. Even the fictitious couples falling in love depresses me. I'm so sick of my family trying to draw me into conversation. It's more painful than wallowing in my own misery.

He pulls up a chair and sits beside me.

Damn. Here we go.

"Tell me," he says.

I put down the book and lower my sunglasses. "What?"

"What you're thinking about? Vlad?"

It's the first time anyone's mentioned his name since I

RENEE ROSE

got back. It's always been t*he stronzo Russian* or more colorful Italian obscenities.

Tears pop in my eyes before I can even draw a breath.

Nico's face turns sympathetic. "You love him."

My chin wobbles. I nod.

"He loves you, too."

I look away because it hurts too much to hear. If he loved me so much, why hasn't he come for me? Why didn't he even try to visit me in the hospital in Russia? Or communicate with me since I've been back?

He may love me, but he's definitely let me go.

"I knew it from that first video call," Nico says. "I saw the way he looked at you. And when you said he hadn't hurt you, I knew I was right. If he wanted my money, he would've made it short and sweet. Collected the money and returned you. Or killed you. But he wouldn't take you to Russia to be his bride. That was fascination on his part."

My nose stings. A tear leaks down my face.

"You know about Stockholm Syndrome?"

"Nico, shut up." I glare at him, pulling off my Chanel sunglasses and wiping a tear.

He holds his hands out in surrender. "I'm just saying— your attachment might be that. Or it could be love. Hard to say without seeing him again, I suppose."

My mouth drops open. Heart starts thumping hard.

Is he suggesting what I think he's suggesting? The idea revs every cell in my body back to life.

He reaches into his pocket and pulls out a crumpled envelope. "He sent you a letter. I opened it first to be sure it wouldn't hurt you."

"Asshole!" I snatch up the envelope. "You don't get to read my mail."

Sondra looks over from the water, surprised at my raised voice. I'm sure she doesn't often hear anyone speak that way to Nico. He's the type who rules his casino with an iron fist, slaying errant employees with just a look.

Right now he's giving me the totally unapologetic, *I do what I want because I'm in charge* face.

I glower at him, but it's not really the fact that he read the letter. It's the effect of holding a letter from Vlad in my hand that has my emotions swirling. I stand up and gather my things, shoving the letter in my purse. No way I'm reading it with him sitting there studying me, even if he already knows what it says.

"Okay," Nico says, also standing. "If you need to see him, we'll arrange it. You know, for closure or whatever."

I go still, considering this offer.

Closure. I'm definitely missing closure.

But I'm not sure that's even what I want.

But yeah, the mere suggestion of seeing Vlad again has my heart racing.

I swallow and nod. "Okay, thanks." Suddenly sorry for my outburst, I lean over for a cheek kiss. "Good night, Nico."

"It's not bedtime," he observes.

"I'm going to tutor Mika, he should just be waking up." I look at my phone. "I'll call down for dinner."

"All right. Make sure you do," he calls to my retreating back. "I see you didn't touch this salad."

I roll my eyes. "I already have one mother, don't need another," I call back.

I take the elevator to my floor and let myself in the room. I pull out the letter and hold it with trembling fingers.

But I'm not ready to open it. Because once I've read it, it will be over. My only contact with Vlad.

And I don't want it to be over.

So I slip the unread letter under my pillow to read before I go to bed, then order a burger and fries from room service.

Mika video calls me right at 7:30 p.m.—6:30 a.m. his time. He must set his alarm to wake up early enough for this. It's very sweet.

The whole time we've been talking, we've stuck to his studies. I don't mention Vlad. He doesn't mention Vlad. I guess I feel like hearing anything would kill me.

Tonight, it feels different, though. Now that Nico opened the floodgates by bringing him up. Bringing me the letter.

Now that Vlad is fresh in my mind and the idea of seeing him is dangling in front of me.

"Hey, Mika," I greet him, sitting down at my desk and adjusting the laptop screen to see him. His hair is rumpled and he still looks sleepy. "I graded your homework and sent it back to you. Open it up and we'll go through it together."

He clicks around on the computer and then nods when he's ready.

I go through his English lesson, then math and science.

"Mika?" I ask when we're through.

"*Da?*"

I rub my lips together, my heart starting to drum again. "How is Vlad?" My voice sounds strangled.

To my horror, Mika's face turns haunted. He shakes his head. "Not good."

I sit forward. "What do you mean not good?"

He shrugs, like usual. "Not good. He…" He glances toward the door. When he turns back, he screws his face up. "He's had trouble—since the surgery." He motions to his back. "It didn't heal right. He's pretty sick."

"*What?* Christ, Mika, why didn't you tell me this sooner?" My blood slams through my veins double-time. "Oh my God, has he been to the doctors? What are they doing for him?"

Mika appears slightly alarmed by my reaction. "Well… I don't know exactly."

"Of course you don't." I tap my lips. "Where is he now? At home? Are you in Volgograd?" It's a stupid question. I know they're in Volgograd because I can see Mika's room in the background. I'm just in panic mode now.

"Yes. I think maybe you should come," Mika says. "Take care of him until he gets better. I mean, if you are well now."

My nose burns. "Yeah, I'm better. I'm much better, actually." I can't believe Vlad is suffering because he gave his kidney to me. The thought horrifies me. All this time I thought he hadn't contacted me because he was through with me. Like he always said he would be eventually. Or because he wanted to grant me the freedom I continuously demanded. Not because he was unwell. Because he had complications as a result of saving my life.

Jesus.

"Okay, Mika. I'm going to look into coming out there. Don't say anything to Vlad, okay?" I know all about alpha males not wanting to show weakness. He probably wouldn't want me to see him like that.

Mika appears greatly relieved. He nods quickly. "I won't. Will you really come? When?"

"I don't know. I'll look into it now and get back to you. Remember—don't say anything."

"I won't," Mika swears.

When I end the video call, I'm suddenly famished. When I got back to the States, my family insisted on putting me on an insulin pump which continuously delivers the medicine, so I don't have to do shots anymore and my blood sugar remains steady. I hate it—it makes me feel weak and fragile and I can't stand having something attached to my body.

Maybe I just miss Vlad taking care of me.

The whole time I eat my dinner and get ready for bed, I'm thinking about the letter under my pillow. Finally, when I can't stand it a moment longer, I pull it out and read it.

It's written in longhand—funny that my tech-savvy Russian didn't just send me an email. How very old-fashioned of him.

DEAR ALESSIA,

I'm sorry.

For everything. For abducting you and bringing you to Russia. Keeping you from your family, whom you love so dearly. For not being there to check your blood sugar the night your kidney failed.

But especially for losing my temper outside Victor's. Forgive me. I lumped you in with Sabina, but you two are nothing alike. She cares only for herself. You care for everyone around you. You bring love and joy everywhere you go, and I miss your beautiful face every day.

I make no claim on you. You are free, of course. I just wanted you to know I suffer everyday knowing I hurt you. If I could take it back, I would, zaika.

Please take good care of yourself.

You have my kidney, but also my heart.

I only beg that you do not hate me.

Yours,

Vlad

I WIPE MY WET CHEEKS. It's perfect. Simple and direct. He said everything I needed to hear.

And he's unwell.

I pick up my cell and call Nico.

"Alessia."

"I'm going to Russia."

I hear Nico sigh. "Not alone, you're not."

"Actually, yes." I've thought it over. I remember what Vlad said. And I don't think he would purposely hurt my brothers if they showed up in Russia, but he may still have orders in place from before. And I'm not planning on telling him I'm coming. "It's not safe for you."

"Oh, and it's safe for you?" Nico demands.

"Completely." I'm not sure it's true. I know I'm safe with Vlad. I don't know about the rest of the brotherhood, but I'm willing to bank on Vlad's power getting me safe passage to him.

Nico curses in Italian—a long string of impressive profanity. Then he says, "Not without clearance from the nephrologist. You call him first. And if he does give you clearance, I need to hear from you twice a day or I'm coming out there to get you. *Capiche*?"

"I'm booking a ticket to Volgograd now," I tell him. "I'll text you the details."

CHAPTER 20

 *lessia*

I HAVE a million worries in my mind, but it's like my body didn't get the message. It's celebrating the whole trip to Volgograd. I just feel light. Happy. Fluttery.

Mika gave me the address and told me exactly what to say to the cab driver to get there. He also sent it in Russian text, and I printed it out to show the guy in case my accent sucked.

I get there in the afternoon. There are fewer guards than he had when I was there—I guess they were to keep me prisoner. I just see one guy outside when I pull up and he nods, like he recognizes me.

Mika comes running out, then stops and shoves his hands in his pockets, awkward-like.

"Come here and give me a hug," I demand, and he shoots forward. "You grew." I laugh, ruffling his hair.

It feels so good to be back. Everything about the estate feels good to me. Truthfully, I never felt like a prisoner here. Just a restricted guest. It's even good to see Zoya's dour face.

"Where's Vlad?" I ask. Oh God, is he completely laid up in bed? How long has he been this way?

"He's at the lake. You should go to him. Help him," Mika says, taking my purse from me. Yegor has already taken my suitcase.

Grazie a Madonna. At least he's not bed-ridden. I head off down the path I took with him so many times. My favorite part of every day I was there. The park bench is still there at the halfway mark. I stop and rest. I may be back to exercising, but I'm still weak. Does Vlad have to use it now?

I hurry forward, excitement and nervousness warring. When I get to the lake, I'm stunned to see Vlad's muscled body cutting through the water.

He's swimming. In the cold lake.

He's beautiful. And perfectly healthy.

He climbs out and picks up a towel from the grass, drying his face. His body is muscled and fit. When he lowers the towel from his face, he sees me.

"Alessia!" His deep voice comes out as a shout.

My heart jumps up into my throat.

But then a leggy blonde stands up from the swing, and my stomach drops to my feet.

No. No fucking way. I did not come all this way to be humiliated by Vlad's new lover.

I stumble back.

"No." Vlad starts running toward me.

My brain has already shut off. I'm in flight or fight mode, I guess, because like a hunted prey animal, I turn and run.

"Alessia! Stop. Wait!"

If I had any doubt at all about his recovery from surgery, it disappears when he overtakes me in about five seconds flat.

He catches me around my waist and lifts my feet from the ground. "Wait. Alessia. She's the nanny. For Lara—the baby. She's the nanny. Don't run."

The fight goes out of me and I go limp in his arms. He lowers my feet to the ground and turns me to face him, still holding me up with an arm banded around my waist. "There's no other woman, *zaika*." He brushes my hair back, then cradles my face with both hands. "There will never be anyone but you." He's kissing me before I can answer. Like he can't wait to taste me. Like we're long lost lovers, dying to be in each other's arms.

Which I guess we are.

My knees go weak as he tastes me, slanting his mouth over mine with more tenderness than he ever showed me before. He takes his time, too. Exploring my lips thoroughly before licking into them, his tongue stroking, probing.

It's the kiss of the century.

"You came," he says with wonder, stroking my cheek with his thumb.

"Yeah, well—" I'm breathless. Still upset over the nanny, even though it's been explained. "Mika said you hadn't healed. But clearly he lied."

Vlad touches the scar on his abdomen, his face growing sober. "I haven't healed," he says.

I get dizzy, realizing he's not talking about the surgery. "Have you?"

I shake my head.

He kisses me again, like a question. Then he picks me up to straddle his waist and walks toward the house. Behind him, I see the nanny hurrying after us, carrying his baby.

He has a baby.

And he took responsibility for her.

My chest fills with warmth. I wrap my arms around his neck.

After a few moments, I realize he's going to carry me the whole way back. "You can put me down." I laugh. "I'm still recovering, but I don't get so out of breath now. Thanks to you—thanks to your kidney."

"I'm not putting you down." There's a stubborn edge to his voice.

I smile.

"I'm sorry for how I treated you. At Victor's." He looks around me to see where he's going.

I weave my fingers into his hair. "I know. I got your letter. Thank you."

Vlad

I'VE NEVER BEEN a religious man. I've never put much

stock in words like holy or sacred. But as I lay my beautiful bride out on our bed, it's with a reverence beyond any spiritual realm.

And she lets me.

I undress her slowly, piece by piece, and she watches, lashes down, belly fluttering, lips parted.

She came here of her own free will.

That, to me, is a miracle worthy of bent knees.

She's not submitting to my will this time, she's offering herself up. It's different. And special and a moment I will never, ever forget.

"What is this?" She's wearing some kind of medical device that made her cringe and blush when I uncovered it.

"Insulin pump. I'll take it off. I hate it."

I tip my head, watching how she takes it off, noting everything so I can help her with it next time. "Seems like a good idea."

She shrugs. "I'd rather have you monitoring me."

And that's when I do drop to my knees. Only on the bed, but still. The words inspire nothing short of a spiritual awakening.

I kiss up her inner thighs, flick my tongue across the flat plane of her belly. I take one pebbled nipple into my mouth. She arches up, moaning softly.

She's a goddess.

The divine feminine.

She is *woman* the way I never saw females before. Pure and potent and life-giving.

"You came," I murmur in awe again. I still can't believe this miracle.

"I'm here," she affirms.

I cup her mons as I move to the other nipple. She's wet and slick and ready for me.

"Beautiful, beautiful woman," I chant. It's a holy rite. Me, worshipping her body.

I scoot back down and push her knees open, feast between her legs. Her juices dribble onto my tongue as I trace her inner lips, suck her swollen clit.

"Tell me something, *zaika,*" I murmur, cupping her ass with both hands to hold her in place as I lick more aggressively.

She cries out, pumps her hips. "What is it, Vlad?"

"Are you here to stay? Or is this just a visit?" I don't know why I ask now. Why I would ruin such a beautiful moment.

But I have to know. Will this be my last time with her? Or is this our new beginning?

"Not to stay," she pants and my heart sinks, even though I suspected that would be her answer.

"I don't want to be away from my family, Vlad. Two of my brothers are expecting babies this fall."

"I see." My voice is strangled, but I'm not going to stop. Not going to give her any less than God and Mother Earth.

"Come back to the States with me, Vlad," she urges, using my hair to tug my face away from her beautiful pussy.

I rise up over her and unzip my jeans, find a condom and roll it on. "I have Mika now," I warn. "And Lara, the baby." I rub the head of my cock over her entrance.

She takes my cock and guides me in, moaning softly.

I fill her, rocking slowly until I'm seated, then easing back.

"I love Mika. And you know I love babies."

I brace my hands beside her head and pump slowly in and out. It's still a religious experience for me, every sensation feeding the sense of oneness. My belief that all is right in the world.

"Vlad?"

I lean my forehead against hers, thrusting a little harder now. "Alessia."

"You haven't answered me."

"The answer is *yes*. Always. To anything you ask of me, *zaika*. I want to be yours. Any way you'll have me."

Her head drops back, eyes close as the sweetest moans comes from her lips. Like she, too, is in ecstatic revelation.

And seeing her like that pushes me over the edge. I shift to white-knuckle the headboard and pump in hard, each thrust a punctuation mark on my promise to her.

I am yours.

Anything you ask of me.

The answer is yes.

She opens her mouth, thrusts her breasts toward the ceiling.

My balls draw up tight, thighs shake. She braces her hands against the headboard, crying out with each thrust.

"I'm not going to last," I grit.

"What are you waiting for?"

I reach nirvana the split second before I come. Alessia follows, hooking her legs around my back and pulling me in deeper, the tight muscles of her pussy pulsing through our release.

"Vlad?" she asks, breathless, arms twining around my neck.

"What is it, *printsessa*?"

"Are we still married?"

I lean on my forearms and nip at her lips. "Yes." I couldn't bring myself to dissolve the marriage, even though I knew it was the right thing to do.

"What happens when you grow tired of me?"

My heart squeezes. Did it bother her when I said that? "That's an impossibility," I tell her. "A lie I told to convince myself I could let you go."

She squirms under me, encouraging me to keep up the slow post-orgasm fucking. "I want a second wedding. An American wedding, with my family."

I go still and she shifts to take me deeper. I have to swallow back the lump in my throat. "You want to marry me?"

"Again. Yes."

I cover her face with kisses, humbled by how easily she surrenders her heart. Her life.

To me.

"Whatever you want, *zaika*. It's yours. Believe it."

"Mmm," she hums softly, pulling me into her so I have to roll us both to the side to keep from crushing her. "I want to hold your baby."

I lean up on an elbow and smile. "Our baby… if you want. Will you adopt her?"

She blinks back tears. "I'd like that. Will you adopt Mika?"

"Yes. I already had papers drawn up for it, but I was waiting for the right moment to talk to him."

"Let's go tell him now." She pushes up to sit and scrambles off the bed. "He's the one who tricked me into coming here."

I didn't want to leave the sanctity of our bed, but seeing her enthusiasm is enough to motivate me.

It won't just be about the two of us. We'll be a family, and there's a sanctity to that, too.

Something Alessia's experienced but I never have. Something I want to give my children.

 *lessia*

VLAD FOLDS me over the side of the bed and smacks my ass. I've spent three wonderful days in Volgograd spending time with Mika, playing with the baby and lying in bed with Vlad. Oh and petting kitties. He kept all five of them, and they roam around the mansion like they own the place.

Tonight, though, he's not quite as reverential.

A little bossy.

The alpha male is showing.

Good thing I like it.

"Ow, what's that for?"

"That, *printsessa*, is for not watching your blood sugar in Moscow." He smacks my ass again. "You didn't think you'd avoid punishment, did you?"

"Isn't there a statute of limitations on it or something? That was three months ago."

He picks up my hands and pins them to my lower back. Then he delivers a flurry of hard spanks. I gasp at the sting.

"What did I tell you would happen if you took risks with your health again?"

"You said if I left the house without insulin," I correct. "I didn't."

He delivers three hard smacks, all in the same place. "So you *do* remember?"

Oh, I remember. He told me he'd fuck my ass raw.

The thought both thrills and terrifies me.

"I remember." My voice sounds small.

One of his digits slides between my ass cheeks and massages my back hole. "When I make a promise of retribution, I deliver."

A shiver runs up my spine.

I know too well that it's true.

"Spread your legs wider."

I obey.

He spanks between my legs, getting me wet and swollen and halfway desperate. Just when I'm about to come, he shifts and starts spanking my ass again.

"No," I moan. "Please, Vlad."

"Please what, *printsessa*?"

I can't say it.

"Tell me what's going to happen."

"You're going to f-fuck me," I manage. He's rubbing my clit now, making me dance under his firm touch.

"Where am I going to fuck you?"

"Please, Vlad," I try again.

He slaps my ass. "Where am I going to fuck you?"

"In my ass!" I can't believe it, but I'm actually growing needy for it. Like I can't wait for him to get started.

"That's right," he purrs. "Don't move, *zaika*." He walks away and returns with a bottle of lubricant, which he dribbles over my fluttering anus.

My breath is short, body flushes all over with heat.

When he nudges my anus with the head of his cock, I moan.

"Open for it, Alessia."

I don't know what that means, but he applies steady pressure.

"Deep breath in."

I obey.

"Exhale."

He pushes in on the exhale and I squeeze at the stretching sensation.

"Relax, *zaika*. Breathe." He doesn't move for a moment, then eases in a little more, until he's past the head. And then he's fully seated, filling me, prying me wide.

It's hot and humiliating and feels way better than it should. There's a little pain, yes, but also pleasure. Embarrassing pleasure.

He goes slow, sliding in and out as I moan and whimper. It's intense. So intense.

He pushes in and stays there as he reaches around and insinuates one hand under my hips. The moment he rubs my clit, pleasure blooms. Still pressing on it, he resumes his plunder, claiming my ass the way he's claimed all the rest of me.

I get louder, both wanting him to go on and retreat at the same time.

He goes on, picking up speed.

My pleasure grows, almost eclipsing the discomfort.

"Yes," I croak. "More. Please, Vlad."

"Beg, *zaika*."

"Please, please, please." I'm helpless not to beg. I need to come. And I also want it to be over.

He adds more lube and it gets better. Much better.

"Yes," I babble. "Please, Vlad."

"Please what?" He's pumping faster, gripping my waist to hold me in place.

"Please fuck me. Please let me come."

He groans and plows even harder, bumping my ass with his hips.

We both cry out when he comes, burying himself deep and working his fingers over my clit.

I come, too, only my muscles can't squeeze because he's stretching me wide. He shoves a few fingers in my pussy, which satisfies my craving for a big finish.

And then he turns sweet again, kissing my back and my neck as we both catch our breaths.

"I told you you'd beg," he murmurs, lips against my ear.

I laugh, because he's right. He told me. I begged. And yet even when he's on top, dominating me, punishing me, I always feel like the winner.

Maybe that's what love is all about.

 *lad*

I SIT at our dining table watching the best view imaginable.

Alessia and Lara splash in the pool, their afternoon ritual. Sondra and her new infant are in the pool, too, having a baby playdate. Junior and Desiree have even flown out from Chicago with their children a couple times to get the cousins together. The joyful sound of baby talk from both the babies and the mothers soothes me on a level I didn't know required soothing.

Mika seems to feel the same way. He looks up occasionally from his studies to watch. Alessia tried to get him to go to school in Las Vegas, but he's steadfastly refused, so he's still homeschooled for now.

She thinks he might change his mind by high school, but either way is okay. He's a good kid. He takes out the trash for Zoya and plays with the baby. Yes, we moved the entire household here—Zoya, Yegor and the five cats.

Alessia insisted, and she gets whatever she wants.

She also wanted to give Mika a puppy for his birthday, so we have a sweet and slobbery Dalmatian underfoot as well. It was worth it to watch Mika's heart open to his new best friend. Alessia climbs out of the pool, and I get up to meet her with a giant towel. Lara smiles and coos at me, waving her tiny fists in the air with joy. I help Alessia dry her off, then take her and give my wife a kiss. Alessia turns to help Sondra with Nico, Jr., her newborn, a big healthy boy full of vigor and life.

The women get together for baby playdates at least once a week and my brothers-in-law have offered me a grudging respect. I'm sure they'd be quick to beat me to a pulp if I ever upset their sister, though.

Victor let me leave Russia, but only because I promised I was diversifying our interests by pursuing the Tacone participation.

Fortunately, Nico's been willing to participate in my laundering scheme for tax savings, so it's worked out. I still have the sense that the shoe may drop at some point. I never expected happiness. Never even pursued it. So now that I have something to live for, I'm fiercely protective of my wife and children. Which Alessia doesn't seem to mind. She's okay with bossy and controlling. Her body comes alive with my dominance.

I just make sure to treat her like the princess she is and she gives me what I hold dearest—her heart.

***

Turn the page to read an excerpt from the next book in the series, *Dead Man's Hand.*

I hope you enjoyed **His Queen of Clubs**. If you loved it, please consider reviewing it or recommending to a friend—your reviews help indie authors so much.

Want more *Vegas Underground*? Read Nico and Sondra's book **King of Diamonds**, Stefano and Corey's book, **Jack of Spades**, Jenna and Alex's short story, *Mafia Daddy,* Tony and Pepper's book **Ace of Hearts,** Junior and Desiree's story **Joker's Wild** and sign up for my mailing list to get word of the release of Marissa and Gio's book *Dead Man's Hand.*

—Sɪɢɴ **up for my mailing list**: http://owned.gr8.com.

--**Get text alerts of my new releases** by Texting: EZLXP55001 to 474747

--**Join Renee's Romper Room**, my Facebook reader group by emailing me with the email you use for Facebook. It's a secret group (because we discuss kink) so I have to send you an invite to join.

WANT MORE?

Please enjoy this excerpt from *Dead Man's Hand* - Book Seven in the Vegas Underground Series

Chapter One - Dead Man's Hand

Marissa

Some things you can't forget. You can't unsee. Can't unhear.

Blood all over these floors. The sound of gunshots. The way my heart stopped when Junior Tacone pointed that gun at me, deciding whether to let me live or die.

I hate this time of day when the customers thin out, business gets slow and I only have time to remember.

It's been six months since the battle between the Russian and Sicilian mafia went down in Caffe Milano and I'm still jumpy as hell. Still examining every customer who comes in, praying he's not Russian mafia come for revenge. Or to shake me down for information on how to find the Tacones.

But they haven't come. No one ever came except the Tacones with their window repair guys and a large enough amount of money to upgrade our whole kitchen. Which was good because our walk-in cooler was inches away from dying and this place hasn't had a remodel since my grandparents opened it in the 1940s.

There once was a time when this deli was the cornerstone of Cicero. And in a way, it still is. Especially with the old-timers. But we don't make the kind of money it takes to keep up with rent increases and modernizations. My grandparents were in a world of debt when I took over the business-end of things, and I've definitely improved the situation a lot, but there isn't money to do the kinds of things I dream about doing here. And I have to work a second job just to pay my own bills.

Of course I like that job much more than this one.

Sometimes I almost wish the shooting had put Caffe Milano out of business. Ended my obligation to grind out this familial obligation.

But that's mean of me. My grandparents raised me and I owe them everything. This deli is their entire world and they're getting too old to run it. Which means until they die, it will be my entire world, too.

I pull a bowl of pasta salad from the deli case to put in the walk-in overnight. When I come back, I freeze.

At first I think it's Junior Tacone standing at my deli counter. I'm not afraid of him, exactly, but he's the man who haunts my nightmares. He's the guy who went gangster on my place and gunned down six guys. And who am I kidding, I am downright terrified of the man.

It's not Junior, though. It's Gio Tacone, the one who took a bullet out on the sidewalk. The man I thought was dead.

"Mr. Tacone!" I curse myself for sounding breathless.

"Gio," he corrects. "Marissa. How are you?"

He knows my name!

That's more than I can say for Junior, the current head of the family. And I wish it didn't do fluttery things to my insides, but it does. Gio rests a forearm on the counter and pins me with a hazel gaze.

He is pure man-candy. With those chiseled good looks, he could easily have been an actor or model and he has the charming personality to match. I never heard if he made it. I checked the newspapers and Googled his name after the shooting, and there weren't any reports of his death, but I saw him take a bullet with my own eyes.

I tried to warn Junior, but it was too late. The ambush happened.

And I've been sleepless with guilt ever since.

"You're alive. I mean, you made it. I'm so glad." I wave my hand and sound like an idiot.

Gio catches my wrist, stilling my hand in the air. My fingers tremble in the space between us. "Why are you shaking, baby girl? You scared of me?"

"No!" I pull my hand away. "I'm just jumpy. You know—since... what happened. And you startled me."

His gaze penetrates, like he knows there's more to it than that and he wants to know it all. A curious shifting happens in my chest.

I tuck an errant strand of hair behind my ear to cover my mounting discomfort.

"You have nightmares?" He guesses, like he's read my mind.

I give a single nod. Then it occurs to me how he knows. "Do you?"

I don't expect him to admit it if he does. I come from an Italian family. I know the men don't admit weakness.

So I'm surprised when he says, "Fuck, yeah. All the time." He touches the place where the bullet must've gone in.

"Wow," I say, like I'm surprised.

He flashes a panty-melting grin. "What, you think real men don't have nightmares?"

"Maybe not the men in your line of work."

He arches a brow, suddenly the stern enforcer, and my heart starts to thump.

"Sorry. I shouldn't have said that, I guess."

He gives a half-shrug, like he's agreeing but letting it go. "I didn't come here to ride your ass, I came to check in on you. Make sure you're okay." He blinks those dark curly lashes that would be feminine except for the manly square jaw and aquiline nose. "Sounds like you're having a hard time."

The danger bell starts tolling in my head.

Never accept a favor from the Tacones. You'll pay for it for the rest of your life.

That's what my grandfather used to always lament. He'd borrowed from Santo Tacone's father to start his business back in the forties and it took him sixty years to pay off. But pay it off he did, and he was damn proud of it, too.

"I'm fine. We're fine. But I'd appreciate it if you'd hold your business meetings somewhere else in the future." I don't know what made me say it. You don't piss off a mob boss by insulting him or making demands. I definitely could've found a nicer way to make my request.

"Agreed. We didn't expect trouble. Junior was real sorry about what happened to this place."

"Junior pointed a gun at my head." I didn't mean to say that, either, but the words tumble out and crash between us.

"Junior would never hurt you." He says it so immediately I know he believes it's true. But he hadn't seen what I saw. That moment of hesitation. The murmuring of his man beside him that I'm a witness.

He thought about killing me.

And then decided not to.

He catches my hand again and holds it, stroking the back of it with his thumb. "That's why you're jumpy, huh? I'm sorry you got scared, but I promise you, you're safe. This place is under our protection."

"Maybe it would be better if it wasn't. You know, if you just left us alone."

If I didn't know better, I would say my words hurt Gio rather than pissing him off. But he just shrugs. "Sorry, baby girl. You can't get rid of us. And you're on my watch now. Which means you're perfectly safe."

I want to tell him I'm not his baby girl and he can take his protection and fuck off, but I'm not insane. Also, some traitorous part of me wants him to keep stroking my hand, keep studying me like I'm the most interesting person he's seen all day.

But I know all that's a lie.

Gio's a player. And my body's response to his presence is dangerous.

Gio abandons my hand in favor of cupping my chin. "You're mad. I get it. I'll let you show me a little claw today. But we paid restitution to your family and will honor our commitments to this neighborhood and to Caffe Milano."

His touch is commanding and firm, but still gentle. It makes the flutters in my belly grow more wild.

"Gio," I murmur, turning my face away from him and out of his hand. My nipples are hard, rubbing against the inside of my bra.

He pulls a hundred dollar bill out of his pocket and drops in on the counter. "Give me two of those cannoli." He points to the case.

I obey wordlessly and tuck the hundred in my apron pocket, not bothering to offer him change. I figure if he used a hundred, it was because he wanted to throw his money around and I'm going to let him do it.

He smirks a little as he takes the plate with the cannoli and sits down at a table in the caffe to eat them.

Fuck. I am so screwed.

Gio Tacone just decided to make me his pet project. Which means the chances of him ending up owning me just shot sky high.

WANT FREE RENEE ROSE BOOKS?

Click here to sign up for Renee Rose's newsletter and receive a free copy of *Theirs to Protect, Owned by the Marine, Theirs to Punish, The Alpha's Punishment, Disobedience at the Dressmaker's* and *Her Billionaire Boss*. In addition to the free stories, you will also get special pricing, exclusive previews and news of new releases.

ABOUT RENEE ROSE

USA TODAY BESTSELLING AUTHOR RENEE ROSE loves a dominant, dirty-talking alpha hero! She's sold over a half million copies of steamy romance with varying levels of kink. Her books have been featured in USA Today's *Happily Ever After* and *Popsugar*. Named Eroticon USA's Next Top Erotic Author in 2013, she has also won *Spunky and Sassy's* Favorite Sci-Fi and Anthology author, *The Romance Reviews* Best Historical Romance, and *Spanking Romance Reviews'* Best Sci-fi, Paranormal, Historical, Erotic, Ageplay and favorite couple and author. She's hit the *USA Today* list five times with various anthologies.

Please follow her on:
   Bookbub | Goodreads | Instagram

Renee loves to connect with readers!
www.reneeroseromance.com
reneeroseauthor@gmail.com

OTHER TITLES BY RENEE ROSE

Vegas Underground Mafia Romance

King of Diamonds

Mafia Daddy

Jack of Spades

Ace of Hearts

Joker's Wild

Queen of Clubs (coming soon)

More Mafia Romance

The Russian

The Don's Daughter

Mob Mistress

The Bossman

Contemporary

Black Light: Celebrity Roulette

Blaze: A Firefighter Daddy Romance

Black Light: Roulette Redux

Her Royal Master

The Russian

Black Light: Valentine Roulette

Theirs to Protect

The Alpha's Punishment

Other Paranormals

His Captive Mortal

Deathless Love

Deathless Discipline

The Winter Storm: An Ever After Chronicle

Sci-Fi

Zandian Masters Series

His Human Slave

His Human Prisoner

Training His Human

His Human Rebel

His Human Vessel

His Mate and Master

Zandian Pet

Their Zandian Mate

His Human Possession

Zandian Brides (Reverse Harem)

Night of the Zandians

Bought by the Zandians

Mastered by the Zandians

Zandian Lights

The Hand of Vengeance

Her Alien Masters

Regency

The Darlington Incident

Humbled

The Reddington Scandal

The Westerfield Affair

Pleasing the Colonel

Western

His Little Lapis

The Devil of Whiskey Row

The Outlaw's Bride

Medieval

Mercenary

Medieval Discipline

Lords and Ladies

The Knight's Prisoner

Betrothed

Held for Ransom

The Knight's Seduction

The Conquered Brides (5 book box set)

Renaissance

Renaissance Discipline

Ageplay

Stepbrother's Rules

Her Hollywood Daddy

His Little Lapis

Black Light: Valentine's Roulette (Broken)

BDSM under the name Darling Adams

Medical Play

Yes, Doctor

Master/Slave

Punishing Portia